HEART-STOPPER!

Josie turned and made her way to the table. Sifting impatiently through the magazines and mail order catalogs, she pulled out another square envelope addressed to her.

Another valentine.

Her breath caught in her throat.

Her hands trembled as she tore the envelope open.

This card was heart-shaped. Bright pink. It said, "Hi, Valentine, remember me?" on the front in fancy script.

Reluctantly, Josie opened the card to find the printed message crossed out and a new message printed beneath it, this time in red ballpoint ink:

> This Valentine's Day
> No memories to save.
> The only flowers for you
> Will be on your grave.

Books by R. L. Stine

Available from ARCHWAY Paperbacks

FEAR STREET® SUPER CHILLER

R·L·STINE

Broken Hearts

AN ARCHWAY PAPERBACK
Published by POCKET BOOKS

New York   London   Toronto   Sydney   Tokyo   Singapore

This book is a work of fiction. Names, characters, places and incidents are either the product of the author's imagination or are used fictitiously. Any resemblance to actual events or locales or persons, living or dead, is entirely coincidental.

AN ARCHWAY PAPERBACK *Original*

An Archway Paperback published by
POCKET BOOKS, a division of Simon & Schuster Inc.
1230 Avenue of the Americas, New York, NY 10020

Copyright © 1993 by Parachute Press, Inc.

ISBN: 0-671-78609-1

First Archway Paperback printing February 1993

15   14   13   12   11   10

FEAR STREET is a registered trademark of Parachute Press, Inc.

AN ARCHWAY PAPERBACK and colophon are registered trademarks of Simon & Schuster Inc.

Cover art by Bill Schmidt

Printed in the U.S.A.

IL 7+

PROLOGUE

SEPTEMBER

THE FALL

The day of the terrible accident was bright and clear.

Erica McClain stared out the back window of the car as houses and yards whirred by. A few leaves had started to turn. The passing maples revealed patches of yellow and scarlet among the dusty green leaves. These splashes of color were the only clue that summer was fading.

Melissa Davis turned the car onto Old Mill Road and pushed down hard on the gas. The blue Firebird responded with a roar. "Why are we doing this?" she asked.

"Why not?" Josie McClain replied. She sat in the front beside Melissa, pushing the radio buttons.

"It's a beautiful day to go riding," Rachel McClain added. Rachel, sitting in back beside Erica, leaned forward into the front. "Stop changing the stations," she scolded Josie. "You're driving me crazy."

"I can't find anything good," Josie complained.

"Then put in a tape," Rachel suggested.

"I forgot the tapes," Melissa told her, swerving to pass a slow-moving van.

Josie stubbornly kept pushing the radio buttons.

Erica chuckled to herself. Josie and Rachel, her older sisters, acted so dumb sometimes.

Josie and Rachel were twins, although they didn't look it. Both sixteen, they called themselves the Un-Twins because they were so different.

Rachel had an oval-shaped face with creamy white skin and large olive green eyes. Her pretty face was framed by long copper-colored hair, which she swept straight back over her shoulders, letting it flow down to her waist.

Despite her fiery hair, Rachel was the cool one, the calm one. She had a soft, whispery voice and a confident, deliberate manner. Rachel was beautiful, and she was used to getting what she wanted. She moved easily through life, like a graceful, sure-footed gazelle.

Josie, with her dark brown hair and dark flashing eyes, was moodier, more temperamental, more unpredictable. Even though she and Rachel got along well, Josie worked hard at being different from her twin.

She kept her hair cut short. She always wore long, jangling earrings. She had worked all summer on her tan, while Rachel remained as pale white as ivory.

Rachel loved to shop and liked to dress in the trendiest styles. Josie seldom wore anything but jeans and T-shirts.

The only way you can tell they're sisters, Erica

thought, is that they constantly fight without really getting angry at each other.

Despite their differences, Josie and Rachel had a closeness that Erica envied. She also envied their freedom. Erica was fourteen, but her older sisters treated her as if she were six!

She was genuinely surprised when Rachel had invited her to go horseback riding with them. Maybe, Erica told herself, now that I'm going to be in Shadyside High with them, they'll start to think of me as a person and not a creepy kid.

"Wait till you see the guy at the stable," Josie was telling Melissa. "You know, the guy who gives you your horse. He's a real babe."

"What's his name?" Melissa asked, stopping for a red light. Melissa was pretty with a lively, animated face framed by long, jet black hair.

"Chuck, I think," Josie replied. "I was so busy staring into his blue eyes, I didn't hear his name. When he smiles, he has dimples in both cheeks. You'll have to check them out. I think he was about to ask me out, but a woman got her foot stuck in a stirrup, and he had to go rescue her."

Rachel laughed. "What a romantic story," she said sarcastically. "Don't you ever get tired of chasing after guys?"

"What a question," Josie muttered.

"Erica, do you have a boyfriend?" Melissa asked, raising her eyes to look at Erica's reflection in the rearview mirror.

Erica could feel her face grow hot. She knew she was blushing. "No. Not really," she said quietly, staring out the window. She chewed harder on her bubble gum, blew a small bubble, then sucked it back into her mouth.

"So you're going to be in ninth grade this year?" Melissa said.

"Yeah. I'm finally in high school," Erica replied.

"Hope you don't get Anderson," Melissa said, eyes still raised to the rearview mirror. "He's the pits."

Melissa was Rachel and Josie's age and Josie's best friend, but she'd always been nice to Erica. She always talked to Erica as if she were someone worth knowing, not someone's pesky kid sister. She lived across the street from the McClains on Fear Street, which is how she and Josie got to be friends.

Erica blew another pink bubble, a larger one this time. Too large. It popped and stuck to her chin.

Rachel laughed. "Very mature," she said scornfully, rolling her eyes.

Erica smiled as she struggled to pull the bubble gum off, but she felt hurt. Is Rachel going to make fun of me the rest of my life? she wondered.

The woods they'd been passing suddenly gave way to rolling green meadows behind log rail fences. A weatherbeaten wooden sign proclaimed Shadyside Riding Club.

Melissa slowed the car and turned into the parking lot, the tires throwing up clouds of dust. Beyond the fence Erica could see several horses standing with their heads lowered, nibbling the grass.

A gray clapboard barn stood at the far end of the parking lot. Behind it, Erica could see a dirt trail cut deep into the meadow and lead off to the woods in the far distance.

She pushed Josie's seat forward and climbed out the open door, shielding her eyes from the bright sunlight. "Wait up!" she called. Melissa and her two sisters were already hurrying across the parking lot toward the broad open door of the barn.

"Hey, Chuck! Chuck!" Josie shouted, waving as a blond young man in jeans and a faded blue workshirt stepped into view leading two horses. He stopped to greet them.

As Erica followed the others into the shadow of the barn, her excitement suddenly gave way to nervousness.

"Oh!"

Startled, she cried out, as one of the horses raised its head and whinnied loudly.

I don't want to do this, Erica thought.

The horses suddenly seemed so tall.

Erica wasn't very athletic. Josie was the athlete in their family. She was a champion tennis player, swam like a fish, and loved to ice skate and play soccer and almost any other sport.

Why did I agree to come along? Erica asked herself. She wasn't much of a daredevil. She liked to keep both feet on the ground.

When the carnival came to Shadyside every summer, Rachel and Josie eagerly clambered onto every ride. Erica dreaded them all—especially the one that spun faster and faster until the floor dropped away, leaving everyone pressed against the round wall.

What was the fun in *that?* she always wondered. She just didn't get the point of rides. She couldn't figure out what was supposed to be fun about making yourself so uncomfortable and putting yourself in jeopardy. While her sisters would scream in delight as they whirred and tilted and spun, Erica would close her eyes, sink into herself, and pray for it to be over quickly.

Now, peering behind Chuck at the tall creatures who were snorting and pawing the ground impatiently, Erica thought of the carnival rides and realized that horseback riding was probably going to be the same kind of frightening, unpleasant experience.

She hung back as Melissa, Josie, and Rachel followed Chuck into the barn. She watched them talking and laughing. Chuck was a great-looking guy, she agreed. Josie sure knew how to pick them.

Josie already had a boyfriend—Jerry Jenkman. Everyone called him Jenkman. Josie was talking about breaking up with him. Josie changed boyfriends nearly as often as she changed her socks, Erica thought, chuckling.

She watched Josie put her hand on Chuck's shoulder as she talked to him. "Boys love that," Josie had once confided to Erica. "It makes them think you're really hot for them."

Chuck had led four horses out of their stalls and tethered them. Now he was pulling blankets and saddles off a pile against the barn wall.

As she watched from the doorway, a cold feeling of dread tightened Erica's stomach.

It smells so gross in here, she thought.

Chuck asked the girls if they'd mind saddling their own horses. He flashed them all a dimpled smile as he hurried out of the barn to help some new arrivals.

"Erica, do you want the black one?" Josie called. "Come over here. What are you doing?"

Erica reluctantly made her way across the straw-littered floor to the others. "I—I don't think I'm going to ride," she said, training her eyes on the black horse Melissa was holding by the reins. The horse's eyes widened and its nostrils flared as Erica moved closer.

It looks like a monster, Erica thought fearfully, a dark monster.

"Huh?" Rachel's mouth dropped open in surprise and she brushed a fly off her pale forehead.

"You're not going to ride?" Josie asked impatiently. "Are you sick or something?"

"A stomach ache," Erica muttered, making a face.

"Erica, every time we do something a little fun, you say you have a stomach ache," Josie complained.

Erica chewed hard on her bubble gum. She could feel her face growing hot. She knew she was blushing. Josie was right, she realized. I really need to think of another excuse.

"That's not fair!" she protested. "I can't help it if my stomach hurts."

"We already paid for your horse," Melissa said quietly. Her blue eyes burned into Erica's, as if trying to determine if Erica was telling the truth.

"I'll go get the money back. Then I'll wait for you here," Erica said.

Josie started to protest, but Rachel interrupted her. "That's fine," she said, coming to Erica's defense. "You don't have to ride if you don't want to."

"My stomach really does hurt," Erica lied, holding her stomach for better effect.

"Do you want me to stay with you? Or drive you home?" Rachel offered with genuine concern.

"Rachel, she's just a chicken," Josie muttered, staring accusingly at Erica.

"No, I'm not," Erica insisted. "I want to ride. I really do."

"Erica, none of us is any good at it, if that's what you're worried about," Melissa said, glancing at Josie. "Josie and I have only been riding once before. Don't tell Chuck. We lied to him the last time and said we were experts."

"We'll go slow," Josie offered.

"Maybe I'll feel better in a little bit," Erica told them. "Then I'll catch up to you."

She hated being so frightened, but there wasn't anything she could do about it. Also, the smell from the stable really was making her feel sick.

Josie started to argue some more, but Melissa stopped her. "We're using up our whole hour," Melissa complained, glancing at her watch.

"You're right," Josie quickly agreed, turning away from Erica. "Come on. Saddle up. Hurry." She made her way over to claim the black horse. "See you later, Erica," she called.

A jumble of feelings swept over Erica. She felt relieved. And disappointed in herself. And angry that she hadn't tried to overcome her fear. And grateful that her sisters hadn't insisted she come along. She slumped down on a wooden bench against the wall, crossed her arms over her chest, and tried not to inhale the pungent aromas.

Rachel's horse, a big chestnut-colored gelding with one brown eye and one blue eye, pawed the dirt floor restlessly as Rachel attempted to fasten the saddle's girth. "Could you help me?" Rachel asked Josie, taking a step back. "I'm not sure I'm doing this right."

Josie finished with her horse, then, slapping a fly off her arm, shoved Rachel out of the way to fasten her sister's girth. "I think you pulled it too tight," she said, showing Rachel the girth. "Steady, fella. Steady. What's your problem?" She put a hand on the horse's neck. "You're as nervous as Erica."

"I heard that!" Erica called from the bench.

"Are you feeling better?" Rachel called to her.

"A little," Erica said. "I'll catch up in a little while. Maybe."

"Yeah. Sure," Josie muttered sarcastically. "Did I do Rachel's saddle right, Melissa?"

Melissa had already led her horse outside and mounted it. It was a dappled white and brown Appaloosa with a weary expression. "Looks okay from here," she called in. "Hurry. We're going to spend all our time in the stable yard."

Rachel led her horse out, put her left foot in the stirrup, grabbed the saddlehorn, and started to pull herself up. Her horse shivered, then flicked its tail with a violent *snap*. "Whoa!" she cried out in surprise, slipping back to the ground. "Why'd he do that?"

Josie and Melissa laughed.

"Don't take it personally," Josie teased.

"He was probably bitten by a horsefly or something," Melissa said.

Rachel grabbed the saddlehorn, pushed her foot into the stirrup, and tried again. This time she managed to pull herself all the way up.

"Ta-daa!" she sang out, smiling. With a toss of her head, she sent her long red hair sailing behind her shoulders.

"Where's your helmet?" Melissa asked Rachel.

"Shh! Don't say anything. I hate to wear them. I want to get out of here without anyone noticing."

"Let's go then!" Josie urged, lowering her heels, the reins secure in her hands. Her horse led the way as they trotted along the dirt path toward the trail behind the barn.

"I feel bad about Erica," Melissa said, glancing back toward the stable.

"She's still such a kid," Josie said, shaking her head disapprovingly.

"Give her a break." Rachel bounced awkwardly as her horse pulled ahead of the others. "She just gets frightened sometimes. Whoa. Whoa," she commanded the horse. "What's your hurry?"

"You're right. I shouldn't be so hard on her," Josie said, catching up to Rachel.

"Ninth grade is tough," Melissa said, appearing even tinier and skinnier than usual as she bobbed on top of the horse. "Changing schools and everything."

"Yeah. She's so excited about being in the same

school with us," Josie replied. "Like she doesn't see us enough at home."

"Whoa!" Rachel said to her horse. "What's this horse's name, anyway, Speed Demon?"

"No. Granny Lady!" Josie joked.

All three of them laughed.

Rachel tossed her long hair as her horse trotted ahead of the others.

The narrow dirt trail led through a meadow of tall grass, which swayed gently in the soft breeze. Crickets sent out a steady electric whistle. A small brown animal, a chipmunk maybe, scampered across the path in front of Rachel's horse.

The meadow ended in a line of tall, blue-green evergreens. The path narrowed as it curved through the woods. The tall trees blocked most of the sunlight. The cricket sounds suddenly stopped. The air smelled piney and sweet.

Rachel's horse slowed to a walk. It set its own pace, as if it were entirely in charge. Josie and Melissa slowed their horses to keep pace with hers. "It's so pretty here," Rachel said, her eyes exploring the shadows from the gently shimmering trees.

"I can't believe summer is over," Melissa said, pulling back on her reins.

"It's definitely over," Josie groaned. "I was at the mall yesterday, buying new jeans for school. Half of Shadyside High was there."

"What are you doing tonight?" Melissa asked Josie, changing the subject. "Going out with Jenkman?"

Josie made a face. "Yeah. Probably." A devilish grin spread across her face. "Unless Chuck asks me."

"Give me a *break!*" Melissa exclaimed. "Don't tell me you're breaking up with Jenkman already."

"Why shouldn't she?" Rachel said. "She's been going with him for nearly a month."

"Ha-ha," Josie replied sarcastically. "You're just jealous, Rachel, because I know a lot of guys. You and Luke are like some old married couple."

"We are not," Rachel protested. Her horse began to pick up speed again, trotting almost silently over the pine needle-covered ground.

"How long have you been going with Luke? Since you were in diapers?" Melissa teased Rachel.

"Since we were freshmen," Rachel told her, sticking her tongue out.

"How boring," Josie groaned. She tightened her grip with her legs as her horse picked up speed to catch up with Rachel's.

"Luke is *not* boring!" Rachel insisted, gripping the reins more tightly as she posted out of time with her fast trotting horse. "Take it back, Josie."

"Dave isn't boring either," Melissa offered.

"I can't believe you're still going out with Dave Kinley," Josie said dryly. "How come you go for all my rejects, Melissa?"

Melissa smiled. "You have so many rejects, Josie. It's impossible *not* to!"

Rachel and Melissa laughed. Josie didn't join in.

"You'll dump Dave too," Josie said seriously. "Just like I did. You'll see. He's so immature."

"Everyone is immature according to you," Melissa replied, her smile fading. "But I like Dave. He's kind of wild, but—"

14

"Immature," Josie interrupted.

"There are worse things than being immature," Rachel called back.

"Name ten," Josie joked.

"Let's stop yakking and ride," Melissa urged impatiently. "We can decide who's immature later, okay?"

Josie and Rachel agreed. The three girls rode on in silence, moving single-file along the twisting path, riding between sunlight and shadows under the tall trees.

The only sounds were the whispers of the trees and the steady, gentle thud of hooves. Melissa found herself becoming hypnotized by the rhythmic rocking, the insistent *clip-clip-clip,* the shifting shadows, the darting golden rays of light poking through the dense foliage.

She found herself thinking dreamily about Dave. Josie was wrong about him, Melissa decided. Josie was a good friend, but she was often wrong about people.

Melissa could see why Josie accused Dave of being immature. He had a wild side, an angry side. Dave could be as moody and childish and unpredictable as Josie, Melissa realized.

They obviously couldn't get along because they were too much alike.

They both had their cruel sides too, Melissa thought. Josie had been really cruel to Dave when she had broken up with him.

Dave had been hurt, Melissa knew.

Melissa raised her eyes to glance at Josie, who was

several yards ahead of her on the path. She watched Josie's short dark hair bob up and down in a steady rhythm under her helmet.

Josie didn't seem to care if she hurt boys, Melissa thought. She could be sensitive and caring when she wanted. She had helped Melissa through some bad times, and she was very loving to her sisters Erica and Rachel.

But when she had made up her mind to dump a guy, she dumped him. That was that. As if the guy were some sort of doll or stuffed animal, to be tossed aside.

"Look, a hummingbird!" Rachel called from up ahead, pointing to a low shrub.

Her voice shook Melissa from her thoughts. She turned her eyes to the blue-green blur buzzing above the shrub, its wings fluttering so fast she could barely get the bird in focus.

"It's so tiny. It looks like an insect!" Josie called.

As if insulted by Josie's remark, the hummingbird raised itself up and darted silently away.

The woods suddenly ended and in a flash of harsh afternoon sunlight, the girls found themselves back on flat grassland. The path straightened out and grew wider as it completed its circuit back toward the riding stable.

Melissa saw Rachel, far ahead, yank hard on her reins. "Whoa!" she was calling. "Hey, slow down, horse!"

Rachel turned back to her companions, a troubled expression on her face, her mane of red hair streaming behind her. "I can't make him slow down!" she cried, alarmed.

"Just keep pulling back on the reins!" Melissa advised, shouting over the thudding of the horses' hooves.

"Whoa! Whoa!"

The dog seemed to appear from out of nowhere. It was a large gray dog, a shepherd of some kind. It ran right in front of Rachel's horse.

Melissa didn't see it until Rachel's horse reared up. The horse whinnied in alarm, a hideous, terrifying sound.

It reared up on its hind legs, then quickly lowered its front hooves, dropping its head.

As it came down, Melissa saw Rachel's saddle fly off.

She and Josie both screamed as the saddle flew over the horse's head. Rachel, her arms thrashing the air in frantic surprise, flew with it.

And as the horse's front hooves came back to earth, Rachel hit the ground with a sickening crack.

The dog began to bark ferociously.

The horse whinnied again, its eyes wide with fear, its nostrils flaring as it took off for the barn.

Rachel lay sprawled facedown on the path. She didn't move.

"She landed on her head!" Josie shrieked. "Melissa, Rachel landed on her head!"

"Josie!" Melissa cried, gasping for breath, struggling to keep her horse steady, the ground tilting up around her. "Josie, go get help! Go to the stable! Get help!"

17

Josie didn't react. She stared down at Rachel's unmoving body.

"Josie! Get help!"

But Josie didn't seem to hear Melissa.

"She landed on her head!" Josie repeated, her dark eyes wide with horror. "She landed on her head! She landed on her head!"

PART ONE

THE FOLLOWING FEBRUARY

Chapter 1

A SURPRISE IN
THE MAIL

"Whoa!"

Melissa could feel the horse thundering beneath her.

It felt so solid, so massive, so strong. The hoofbeats thundered through the darkness. The horse was galloping out of control.

Out of control.

She could feel its muscles flex, hear its loud, steady breathing. She could feel its warmth, its heavy sweat.

"Whoa! Please!"

Through the darkness. Out of control.

She couldn't stop it.

Faster it galloped.

She leaned forward, her jet black hair flying behind her, and wrapped her arms around its neck.

"Whoa! Please, whoa!"

Holding on tightly, so tightly she could feel the blood pulsing through the horse's veins, feel it swallow, feel it gulp air as it surged through the night.

"Help me! Somebody, help me!" Melissa screamed.

She lay against the animal's neck, leaning into its solid weight as she bounced wildly, frantically.

Out of control.

"Help me, somebody! I'm going to fall!"

Through the hot darkness.

She could hear each breath the horse took, each pulse of its heart, each thud of its hooves.

"Help me! Help me!"

She could still feel the horse galloping and its banging heartbeats as someone shook her and called her name.

"Melissa, wake up!"

But the horse wouldn't stop.

Even as someone called Melissa's name and tried to shake her awake, the horse wouldn't stop.

Then she opened her eyes, still bouncing, still holding on so tightly, still out of control.

"Melissa, another dream," her mother said softly, peering down at her in the blue-black light of the darkened bedroom, her eyes wet with concern. "Another bad dream, Melissa. Wake up."

"The horse wouldn't stop," Melissa said.

Mrs. Davis wrapped her daughter in a hug. Her nightgown smelled of perfume, tangy and sweet.

My mom feels so cold, Melissa thought, staring wide-eyed but seeing nothing. I guess it's because I'm so very hot.

"The horse wouldn't stop," Melissa whispered, pulling away, sinking back onto her damp pillow. "I was going to fall."

"Five months later and you're still dreaming about horses," Mrs. Davis said softly. She leaned forward and clicked on the bedside lamp.

Melissa squinted against the harsh cone of yellow light. "Yeah. Five months later," she said glumly, finally out of her horrifying dream.

The horse faded into the light. The rhythm of its hooves drowned out by a rush of cold wind through the open bedroom window.

"The same dream over and over," Melissa said, pulling the covers up to her chin. "It's even the same horse."

Her mother stood up, yawning. She crossed the room, the old floorboards creaking under her bare feet, and closed the window.

Melissa could see a half moon high in the sky, split in two by a black wisp of cloud.

"Eventually the dream will go away," Mrs. Davis said softly. She came back beside the bed and stared down at Melissa tenderly.

"It's always the same," Melissa told her, trembling under the covers. "And it's so real."

Her mother leaned down and gently brushed Melissa's thick black hair off her forehead. "Just a nightmare," she said. The words sounded hollow—to both of them.

"The same horse," Melissa muttered, picturing its dark back, its long-haired mane.

"Have you seen Rachel and Josie lately?" Mrs. Davis asked, pulling down the sleeves of her nightgown.

Melissa nodded. "I visit Rachel whenever I can," she said, her voice breaking. "I *think* she's happy to see me. It's really hard to tell. She doesn't say much. Just stares a lot."

Her mother *tsk-tsked,* shaking her head sadly, her eyes wet with tears again.

"Sometimes Rachel seems pretty good," Melissa continued thoughtfully. "Sometimes I think she understands what I'm saying. But then other times, I'm not sure. I mean, sometimes when I visit her, she talks crazy. She doesn't make any sense at all. And sometimes . . . sometimes I don't think she even knows who I am."

"How dreadful," Mrs. Davis said, her voice barely a whisper.

Melissa turned her eyes back to the window. The moon was completely lost in black clouds now.

She pictured the horse again. Felt its throbbing back. She heard its throaty gasps.

"And what about Josie?" her mother asked.

Melissa uttered a loud sigh. "I don't know, Mom. Josie and I just aren't friends anymore."

Mrs. Davis's eyes widened in surprise. She lowered herself to the edge of the bed and brought her face close to Melissa's. "Why, Melissa?"

Melissa had to choke the words out. "Josie blames me. She blames me for Rachel's accident."

Her mother gasped. She squeezed Melissa's hand. "But that's so unfair!" she exclaimed.

Melissa closed her eyes. "I know," she whispered. "I know . . ."

"Steve, stop it! Don't come any closer!" Josie exclaimed.

She backed up, her boots snagging in the shag rug. She eyed Steve Barron warily as he continued to stalk her, a strange smile on his face.

"Come on, stop!" Josie cried, her back colliding with the pine-paneled wall. "What have you got behind your back?"

Steve's grin grew wider. His blue eyes sparkled mischievously. "Nothing," he said softly. "What makes you think I have something behind my back?"

"Steve—" Josie started.

He swung his arm around, revealing the smooth, white snowball in his hand. Before Josie could cry out in protest, he grabbed her by the shoulder and pushed the icy snowball into her face.

"I'll get you!" she cried, laughing and trying to squirm away.

He was laughing so hard she was able to grab the snowball out of his hand. She tried to hit him with it, but it disintegrated, dripping onto the carpet.

"You're not funny!" Josie exclaimed, and wiped her cold, wet hand against his face. "My mom'll kill you for bringing snow in the house."

"She isn't home," Steve said, still holding her shoulder. His eyes lit up. A devilish grin spread across his handsome face. "Hey, she isn't home!" he declared. He lowered his head and pressed his lips against hers. Leaning against the den wall, Josie returned the kiss.

They were interrupted by high-pitched yapping from the doorway. Startled, Josie pushed Steve away.

"Muggy, what's your problem?" she called to the little white terrier, who continued barking in alarm, his stub of a tail wagging frantically. "It's only Steve."

"Boo!" Steve shouted.

The dog yipped and started toward Josie, as if coming to protect her from Steve. But the wet snow on the rug distracted the little dog, and it stopped to sniff it, then lick it.

"How can you stand that little rat?" Steve teased. "Why don't you step on it and put it out of its misery?"

Josie's expression turned to mock outrage. "You're disgusting. How can you say such a horrible thing about Muggy?" She stooped and picked the dog up, wrapping it in a tight hug against her pale blue sweater. "Don't listen to him, Muggy."

The terrier gave Josie's face a fast lick, then thrashed its legs, struggling to escape from her.

"Yuck," Steve said, shaking his head. "You let that rodent lick you? How do you know *what* he's been licking before he came in here?"

"Don't be gross," Josie replied, setting Muggy down gently.

The dog sniffed the snow on the carpet again, then sneezed, before hurrying out of the room.

Josie glanced out the den window. The snow had stopped coming down. The snow-covered front yard glowed like silver under the late-afternoon sun.

Across the street, she could see Melissa's house, patches of snow piled on the windowsills and clinging to the gray shingles. Melissa's blue Firebird was parked in the drive.

Josie turned away from the window. "It's cold in here," she complained, rubbing the arms of her sweater. "I hate this drafty old house."

Steve took a step toward here. "Come here. I'll warm you up."

She started to push him away, then changed her mind and let him kiss her again. She stared into his eyes as they kissed. She didn't like to close her eyes. She liked to watch him.

He's so good-looking, she thought. In an all-American sort of way. Wavy, blond hair. Clear blue eyes. Perfect straight nose. Lopsided grin. Broad shoulders.

How long had she been going with Steve? Ever since she'd dumped Jenkman. That was right after Rachel's accident. Last September. So she and Steve had been seeing each other for almost five months.

That's a long time, Josie thought. For me, anyway. And I'm not the least bit bored with him yet.

What's your secret, Steve? she wondered as she pressed her cold cheek against his warm one. Is it because you bring snowballs into the house? Because I can never guess what you're going to do next?

He stepped away from her and raked a hand back through his blond hair. Then he straightened his maroon and white Shadyside High sweatshirt. "Are we going to the mall, or what?" he asked.

"Yeah. Sure," she replied, untangling a long, dangling earring. She started toward the doorway. "I'll go upstairs and tell Erica we're leaving."

"Is Erica going to give you a hard time?" Steve asked.

"She usually does," Josie said.

She stopped just outside the doorway to the den. The mail had been piled on the narrow table against the wall. She picked up the stack and shuffled through it.

"Hey, something for me," Josie said, pulling out a square envelope. She let the rest of the mail drop back to the table.

"Who's it from?" Steve asked.

Josie shrugged. "I don't know."

She ripped open the envelope and pulled out a greeting card.

She read it silently, then gasped, her hand trembling, her eyes wide with fear.

Chapter 2

HAVE A HEART

"*I*—I don't believe this," Josie stammered, staring at the card.

"What is it?" Steve asked, turning away from the window.

"It's a valentine," Josie replied, holding it up.

"From who? I didn't send you a valentine." He made his way across the room to her.

"It isn't signed," Josie told him. "But it—it's *disgusting.*" She shoved the card into his hand. "Here. Read it."

Steve took the card from her and examined it. There was a satiny red heart on the front.

He opened it up. The printed words had been crossed out with a black marker. Written underneath them in blue ink was a short rhyme.

Steve read it aloud:

"Violets are blue
Roses are red.
On Valentine's Day
Josie will be dead."

Steve stared down at the card for a moment, scanning the rhyme again, silently this time. Then he closed the card and grinned at Josie. "It rhymes okay," he said.

She gave his shoulder a hard shove. "Who cares? Can't you take anything seriously?"

His smile faded. He looked hurt. "You don't think this is serious, *do* you?" he demanded, rubbing his shoulder. "It's too dumb."

Josie pulled the card from his hand and glanced over the handwritten message again. "I don't know *how* to take it," she said. "I mean, it is stupid, but it is a threat."

"It can't be serious," Steve said, putting a hand on her shoulder. "It's just someone's idea of a joke."

"What kind of joke?" Josie demanded heatedly. "I mean, what's the funny part?"

"I don't know. I don't get it," Steve said. He picked the torn envelope up from the table. "No return address." He put the envelope back and turned to her. "So who sent it?"

"I don't know," Josie said, staring at the card. "Probably Jenkman."

"Jenkman?"

"Yeah. Probably. He's such a creep," Josie said, frowning. "He still calls me, still pesters me. He can't believe I broke up with him. He can't believe that I don't want to go out with him again."

"You think he sent this?" Steve asked.

"You should see the way Jenkman stares at me in school," Josie continued. "Like a hungry puppy dog. Mister Pitiful. He follows me, staring at me. Like I'm supposed to feel bad or something. Like I'm supposed to care."

"Calm down," Steve said softly.

"How can I calm down?" Josie snapped. "I broke up with him five months ago. And now he sends me this dumb thing. Is he crazy, or what?"

"You know what I think you should do?" Steve said seriously. "I think you should ignore it."

"Huh? Ignore it?"

"Yeah. Don't mention it to anyone. Pretend you never got it. That's what I'd do."

Josie tossed the card down on the table. "I suppose you're right," she said, sighing. "You're so sensible, Steve."

"That's me," he replied brightly. "Sensible Steve."

She leaned forward and gave him a quick kiss on the cheek.

"Now let's get out of here," he said, smiling. "And no more talk about that stupid valentine."

Josie started to reply. But before she could get a word out, pale white hands reached out from behind her, wrapped themselves around her throat, and started to choke her.

Chapter 3

RESENTMENT

Josie gasped and spun away, breaking loose from her attacker. "Rachel!" she cried. "Don't do that!"

Rachel laughed, her hands still outstretched as if prepared to strangle Josie. Her olive eyes sparkled gleefully.

"Rachel, that wasn't funny. Stop laughing," Josie said firmly.

Obediently, Rachel cut off her laugh, as if a switch had been flipped. Still staring at Josie, she lowered her hands, then shoved them deep into the pockets of the loose-fitting brown corduroy jumper she wore over a pale yellow, long-sleeved T-shirt.

"Erica, where are you?" Josie called angrily. "I thought you were watching Rachel." She rubbed her neck where Rachel had grabbed it.

"Hi, Rachel," Steve said timidly.

Rachel didn't respond.

Erica ran down the stairs, a troubled expression on her face. She was followed by Luke Hoskins. "Here you are," Erica said softly to Rachel. "You got away from us, didn't you?"

"You were supposed to be watching her," Josie said crossly, narrowing her eyes suspiciously at Luke.

Luke was tall and lanky. His shoulders were always stooped, as if he were trying to make himself shorter. He had short, light brown hair, neatly parted on the left and brushed to the side. His slender, nervous face was framed by silver-rimmed glasses. A tiny gold ball glistened in his right earlobe.

He and Rachel had been going together for more than two years before her accident. Since that terrible day, Luke had been a constant visitor in the McClain house. He seemed as devoted to Rachel as before, even though she seldom responded to him in any normal way.

"It's my fault," he admitted to Josie. "Erica and I were talking about something, and we didn't see Rachel leave the bedroom."

"Well, you *know* she can't be out of your sight," Josie scolded shrilly. She rubbed her neck. "She nearly strangled me."

Rachel laughed, tossing her head, her long, red hair catching the light from the ceiling.

"She was just playing with you, Josie," Erica replied heatedly. "You *could* give her a little attention, you know." Erica's voice revealed her bitterness.

Rachel picked up the stack of mail from the table and stared at it as if trying to figure out what it was.

33

"Put that down," Erica said gently, taking the envelopes from Rachel's hands. "No mail for you today." She tenderly placed a hand on Rachel's shoulder.

"No mail for me?" Rachel repeated, her voice nearly a whisper. She turned to Josie. "Brush my hair," she said.

"No, Rachel," Erica replied before Josie could speak. "I just brushed your hair. Upstairs. Remember?"

"Steve and I are going to the mall," Josie interrupted impatiently. "I'll be back in time for dinner."

"But you promised—" Erica wailed angrily.

"If Mom gets home, tell her I'm going to look for that pattern she wanted," Josie said, ignoring Erica's protests.

"Hold on, Josie," Erica insisted, still holding on to Rachel's shoulder. "You promised you'd watch Rachel this afternoon. I *told* you I had to study for my social studies exam."

"Sorry. Some other time," Josie said coldly.

"You said that the *last* time!" Erica complained.

"Brush my hair," Rachel said insistently, seemingly unaware of the argument taking place.

"We just brushed your hair, dear," Erica said softly. Then her expression returned to one of anger as she glared at Josie. "You're always running out and leaving me with Rachel. You and I are supposed to take turns. You know we can't afford help for her during the week."

"I'll take my turn. Don't worry about it," Josie said with a sneer.

"When?" Erica demanded shrilly.

"Brush my hair," Rachel said, her hands jammed back in the pockets of her jumper.

"If you want, we could go to the mall tomorrow," Steve suggested to Josie.

"Shut up," Josie snapped. "We're going now." She pushed past Rachel and Erica to get to the hall closet. "Out of my way. I'm getting my coat."

"This isn't *fair!*" Erica cried. "You stick me with her every day. I have no life, Josie!"

Josie swung back angrily, her eyes aflame, raising a finger to her lips. "Sshhh. Rachel can hear, you know, Erica. Watch what you say. You'll hurt her feelings."

Erica uttered a loud shriek of disgust. "Don't tell *me* about Rachel's feelings!" she screamed. "Since when do *you* care about Rachel's feelings? You haven't spent ten minutes with her since . . . since . . . ."

"That's not true," Josie snapped back, her voice trembling.

"Erica's right," Luke said quietly, stepping up beside Erica. "You really haven't done your share, Josie."

"You keep out of it," Josie replied angrily. "You're not in this family."

"I know that, but I can see what's happening here," Luke said, his expression troubled. "I can see that—"

Muggy interrupted, yapping in his high-pitched squeaky voice, his toenails clicking across the floorboards as he ran up to them.

Josie scooped him up and pressed his black nose against hers. "It's okay, Muggy," she said, holding the dog close to her face. "Did all this shouting upset you? It's okay, doggie."

The dog licked Josie's nose.

Josie glared at Erica. "Look how you upset Muggy."

Erica uttered another cry of disgust. "Josie, you care more about that dumb dog than you do your own sister," she accused.

"That's not true! Take that back!" Josie demanded, holding the terrier against her chest.

"Look!" Rachel said, holding up the stack of envelopes, which she had picked up again. "Mail for me?"

Steve appeared in the doorway behind her. He had gone into the den with Rachel when the yelling began. "She seems fascinated by the mail," he said.

"Mail for me?" Rachel repeated. She held the envelopes high in one hand, showing them to everyone.

"Rachel doesn't get mail anymore," Erica whispered sadly. "Maybe she misses it."

Some of the envelopes fell from Rachel's hand and fluttered to the floor.

Erica dropped to her knees and began to scoop them up. She stopped when the satiny red heart of the valentine caught her eye. "What's this?" she asked Josie, holding it up. "You're getting a valentine five days before the day?"

"Read it," Josie told her sister. "Maybe you can figure out who sent it to me."

"Huh?" Erica's expression was confused. Still on her knees, she opened the card and read the verse aloud:

"Violets are blue
Roses are Red.
On Valentine's Day
Josie will be dead."

Erica glanced up at Josie, even more bewildered now.

To everyone's surprise, Rachel began to laugh uproariously. She laughed so hard she started to cough.

"Rachel, that isn't funny," Erica said softly, staring at the card as she climbed to her feet.

Rachel immediately became silent, but her eyes continued to reveal her merriment. After a few seconds she burst out in high-pitched giggles, covering her mouth as a little girl would.

"This is really gross," Erica told Josie, waving the card in Josie's direction.

"Tell me about it," Josie replied, rolling her eyes.

"Who would send such a horrible thing?" Erica demanded.

"Just one of my many admirers, I guess," Josie said dryly. She pulled her coat from the closet, then grabbed Steve's jacket and tossed it to him. "Let's go," she said, avoiding Erica's stare.

Erica was still holding the valentine open in her hand. She raised her eyes from the card to her sister. "I really don't believe this," she said, shaking her head.

"See you later," Josie said, pulling her coat over her shoulders. Steve followed her down the hall, and a few seconds later the front door closed behind them.

Erica heard Muggy whining and whimpering by the

door. He always did that whenever Josie went away. A few seconds later he gave up. She heard his tiny paws click away in the direction of the living room.

"Brush my hair," Rachel insisted, a strange, unreadable smile on her face. An eerie, ghostlike smile. "Brush my hair."

She looks so pretty in the dim hall light, Erica thought, staring at her older sister. With that beautiful hair and those big, olive eyes and that pale, pale skin. She looks like an angel. She really does.

With her innocent, childlike eyes. And that sad, haunting smile . . .

Erica uttered a loud sob, quickly muffling it with her hand.

No, she thought. I promised myself. I promised myself no more tears. No more crying. No more.

"Brush my hair?" Rachel asked as if she had never made the request before.

"Okay," Erica told her. "Let's just put down this mail and then we'll go back up to your room."

"I don't *believe* Josie," Luke muttered angrily.

His voice startled Erica. She had nearly forgotten he was still there.

He stepped toward her from the shadows of the dim hallway, and she was startled by the bitter expression that twisted his normally placid features.

"I don't *believe* her," he repeated, his eyes wide with anger behind his silver-rimmed glasses. "She should help out."

"I know," Erica said, dropping the mail onto a table in the den, then taking Rachel by the hand.

"She should do her share," Luke continued. "She *was* responsible, after all, for Rachel's accident."

Erica stopped short. She was shocked by Luke's words. She had never heard him talk like this. So angry. So frighteningly angry.

Just then a burst of laughter escaped from Rachel. She pointed at Luke. "You look funny," she told him.

Luke forced a weak smile, but Erica could see that he was still seething.

"Funny," Rachel said, laughing.

Luke forced himself to laugh too, but when he started to laugh, Rachel stopped.

Taking Rachel by the hand, Erica began to lead her to the stairway. Luke followed close behind. In a glance, Erica saw that his bitter expression had returned.

"Why do you say it was Josie's fault?" Erica asked.

"You know," he snapped. "The saddle. Josie fastened Rachel's saddle. She could've killed Rachel. She nearly did. And now Josie doesn't care at all."

They climbed the stairs in silence, Erica too shocked by Luke's words to respond to them.

I had no idea he resented Josie so much, she thought, as she led Rachel to her bedroom. No idea.

No idea that he carries around so much anger.

Of course, he did lose his girlfriend because of the accident. He did lose Rachel.

And he blames Josie for it.

So why does he still come around all the time? Why hasn't he found a new girlfriend? Why does he spend so much time visiting Rachel? Erica wondered.

Sometimes Rachel seems glad to see him, Erica observed. But most of the time she doesn't even remember who he is.

Erica led the way into Rachel's dark bedroom and clicked on the bedside lamp. Rachel took her usual place, sitting on the edge of her double bed, her pale hands pressed against the dark green bedspread. She closed her eyes and waited patiently for Erica to begin brushing out her long, straight hair.

Luke sat down at the chair by Rachel's desk, folding his slender arms over his chest.

Why does he come? Erica asked herself, picking up the hairbrush. If he's so bitter and angry, why does he come?

Then, glancing across the room at Luke, Erica had a chilling thought. He's here for revenge against Josie. Luke is the one who sent the valentine.

Chapter 4

SURPRISE IN THE SNOW

"Is it ever going to stop snowing?" Josie asked herself.

It was Wednesday afternoon. The snow had come down all day, a blizzard of large white flakes adding to the white piles already on the ground.

Josie hitched her backpack up on the shoulder of her blue down jacket and stepped out of the school building. The sky was charcoal gray even though it was only three o'clock. Heavy gray clouds hovered menacingly low.

The front walk hadn't been shoveled, and Josie's boots sank deep into the fresh snow as she made her way toward Park Drive. Swirling wind sent powdery snow flying around her as she walked.

She swung her maroon wool scarf around her neck and pulled it up over her chin. The big trees near the street shook in the breeze, sending down a silent shower of fresh snow.

"Hey, Josie! Wait!"

Recognizing her sister's voice, Josie turned back toward the school.

She watched Erica trying to run, stumbling over the slippery walk, her coat unfastened and flapping out behind her.

She looks like a big clumsy bird trying to take off, Josie thought cruelly. Erica isn't as pretty as Rachel and me, Josie realized, with a bit of sympathy. Her face is too round. Her hair is that mousy light brown. She could lose some weight too.

"Josie, where are you going?" Erica cried breathlessly as she caught up to her sister. Breathing hard, she wrapped her coat more tightly around her without zipping it.

"Erica, what's your problem?" Josie asked. "Why are you screaming like a lunatic? I'm going to meet Steve."

"You can't!" Erica cried. She tried to stamp the snow off her boots, but it was useless.

"Sure, I can," Josie said softly, glancing at the street where several Shadyside High kids were blocking traffic with a spontaneous snowball fight. "I'm meeting him at The Corner." She motioned with her head toward her favorite hangout, a few blocks away.

"But you can't!" Erica insisted shrilly. She started to say more, but someone behind Josie caught her attention. "Look. There's Jenkman," Erica said, lowering her voice. "Over by the side of the school. Trying to get your attention."

"Who cares?" Josie snapped.

"He's coming this way," Erica reported. "He's waving at us."

"Thrills and chills," Josie said sarcastically.

"Hi, Josie!" Jenkman called from a few yards behind her on the walk.

Josie pretended not to hear.

Jenkman came closer. "Josie, how's it going?"

She continued to ignore him.

Erica saw the hurt on Jenkman's face.

"Josie, I just want to talk!" Jenkman said, stepping up beside her.

Josie turned her back on him.

Erica saw Jenkman's face turn bright red. He uttered a loud curse and hurried past them to the street.

"Wow," Erica said, following him with her eyes. "Wow. Was he mad!"

"He's a creep. What do you want?" Josie demanded impatiently. "I'm late."

"You *have* to take care of Rachel this afternoon," Erica said, grabbing the sleeve of Josie's coat. "I told you this morning I have *Brigadoon* tryouts. You know. For the drama club."

"You'll have to try out some other time," Josie said brusquely. She started to pull away from Erica, but Erica held on.

"No way," Erica said angrily.

A gust of wind made the powdery snow swirl all around them. Josie closed her eyes and tried to slip her face down into her wool scarf.

Go away, she thought. Please. Just go away, Erica.

"You're supposed to help take care of Rachel when

43

she gets home from her school," Erica scolded. "You know that, Josie. It's not supposed to be my full-time job."

"I know. Give me a break," Josie said, starting to walk toward the street. "I'll take care of her tomorrow. Promise."

"No. Today!" Erica insisted, following her. "I don't want to miss the tryouts. It's just not fair. This is my first year in high school. It's supposed to be such a big, exciting year for me. And instead—"

"Tomorrow," Josie told her, picking up her pace. "I can't leave Steve waiting there."

"Yes, you can," Erica told her. "You can call and leave a message for him."

"I don't want to," Josie said nastily. She began to jog across the snow.

Erica caught up to her. "I don't believe you, Josie," she cried breathlessly. "I can't believe you don't take more responsibility for Rachel. After all, it *was* your fault—"

Erica stopped herself.

Uttering a silent gasp, she raised her hands to her face, as if trying to hide behind them.

She realized she had gone too far.

She had no right to say that.

She could feel her face grow hot. She knew she was blushing.

She should never have said that. It had just slipped out. Slowly she lowered her hands. Josie was glaring at her.

"I'm—I'm sorry," Erica stammered. "I—I didn't mean . . ."

She waited for Josie to say something.

A loud thud startled her.

To Erica's horror, Josie let out a painful squeal. She watched Josie's eyes go wide, her mouth drop open. Then she crumbled to the snow.

Chapter 5

ANGER

*E*rica stood frozen for a long moment. The world went white, as white as the snow that surrounded her. When the colors returned, she bent to help Josie.

"I'm okay," Josie declared, raising a gloved hand. "Help me up."

Erica heard laughter from behind them. She turned to see Dave Kinley with a snowball in his hand. Melissa Davis was beside him, embarrassment clear on her face. Several other kids, spread out over the school's front lawn and into the street, were tossing snowballs at one another as fast as they could make them.

"A snowball hit me on the back of the neck," Josie told Erica, climbing to her feet. "I was so stunned, I fell." She brushed the clinging snow off her jacket and jeans with both hands.

Then Josie turned angrily to Dave. "You're not funny, Kinley!" she called angrily.

Dave gave her an exaggerated shrug, a wide grin on his face. "Sorry, Josie. My hand slipped!" He laughed at his own feeble excuse. Several other kids laughed too. Melissa turned away, avoiding Josie's stare.

Dave continued to stare back at Josie, the snowball in his hand, as if challenging her.

Josie wanted to say something, but stopped herself. She turned away angrily from Dave and tossed the end of her wool scarf around her neck.

"I'm going," she muttered to Erica and hoisted her backpack to her shoulder. "Why should I waste my breath on that creep?"

"Hey, wait!" Erica cried, slipping on the snow as she tried to chase after her sister.

Erica saw Jenkman then out of the corner of her eye. He was leaning against a tree, half hidden by its snow-patched trunk. She realized he was staring at Josie. Staring at her with the strangest expression on his face.

"Hey, Josie! Stop!" Erica called. When she glanced back, Jenkman had disappeared.

A snowball flew over Erica's head and landed with a soft plop on the snow-covered sidewalk ahead of her.

"I'll stay with Rachel tomorrow!" Josie shouted back without stopping. "I'm late."

"But my tryout!" Erica wailed. She uttered an exasperated groan. Josie pretended not to hear her and continued down the block, half-walking, half-jogging.

Shaking her head, unhappy that she'd have to miss tryouts, Erica headed back to the school to get her backpack. She glanced at her watch and realized she'd have to hurry. Rachel would be home soon.

"What's your problem, Dave?" Melissa asked as soon as Josie and Erica were out of sight.

"Huh? What do you mean?" He grinned at her, his dark eyes flashing.

With long, scraggly black hair down to his collar, small, round eyes, and a bent nose, Dave wasn't exactly handsome. But he had an easy-going, happy-go-lucky attitude, a warm, winning smile, and a great sense of humor. It was his sense of humor and his playfulness that attracted Melissa to him. They'd been going together for nearly six months now.

"Why'd you throw that snowball at Josie?" Melissa demanded.

Dave's grin widened. "Because she was there."

"No, really," Melissa insisted, kicking at the snow with her boot.

"I don't know." Dave struggled to zip his brown leather bomber jacket all the way to the collar. It was a difficult job since he was wearing gloves. "I just hate her. That's all."

Melissa let out a bitter laugh. "I don't think so. I think you still like her." She stared into his eyes as if challenging him.

"Huh? No way!"

"I think you still care about her," Melissa said. "I think you threw that snowball because you wanted to get her attention."

"That's stupid," Dave muttered, glancing away. She

couldn't tell if his cheeks were pink from the cold or from blushing.

"Admit it. You still like her," Melissa insisted.

"No way," he replied heatedly. "After all that Josie's done to me? You know, I'm the first guy who ever dumped her. And she's been on my case ever since."

"*You* dumped *her*?" Melissa exclaimed. "That's not the way Josie tells it. She tells everyone that *she* dumped *you*."

"Whatever," Dave muttered, making a disgusted face. He tossed the snowball he'd been holding down at his feet. "That was months ago," he said. He narrowed his eyes at her. "Why are you sticking up for Josie? She dumped you too."

Dave's words stung. Melissa felt a wave of sadness sweep over her.

"She used to be your best friend," Dave continued, bending to pick up another handful of snow. "Then she dumped you like she dumps everyone else."

"Okay, okay," Melissa snapped. "You're right. Let's forget Josie."

"Fine with me," Dave said, softening his tone. He rounded off the snowball and heaved it at the nearest tree. It made a satisfying *thunk* as it splattered against the trunk.

"I'll never forgive Josie," Melissa said, her voice breaking. "I'll never forgive her for blaming me for Rachel's accident." Melissa couldn't force Josie from her thoughts.

"It's just so unfair," she continued, watching Dave

pack another snowball between his gloves. "Josie acts as if she had nothing to do with it. *She* was the one who fastened the girth on the saddle. Not me. Just because she asked me to check it—"

"Calm down," Dave said, throwing his latest snowball at the tree. This time he missed. "Don't get started."

"You know what Luke Hoskins told me?" Melissa continued, ignoring Dave's suggestion. "Luke told me that Josie is mean to Rachel. She refuses to pay any attention to her, and doesn't spend any time with Rachel at all."

"Does Luke still go over there?" Dave asked, sounding surprised as he slapped his gloves together to get the snow off.

Melissa nodded. "Yeah. Poor guy. He's really messed up. He can't believe that Rachel will never be Rachel again. I ran into him yesterday after school. He was on his way to her house. That's when he told me how awful Josie is being."

Dave sighed bitterly. "Luke and I should form a club. An anti-Josie club. We could get together and swap stories. You remember what happened at Christmas when Josie's dad was going to give me a job in one of his hardware stores. All of a sudden, just before vacation he called and said he couldn't use me. Just like that. So I had no job over the holiday. And I really needed the money. I *know* Josie had something to do with it. I'm *sure* she convinced her dad not to hire me."

Dave's face was bright red now. He quickly made

another snowball and heaved it at a passing truck. It smacked the side of the truck, and the driver honked his horn.

"We've been over that a thousand times," Melissa said, frowning. "You're being totally paranoid. Josie didn't lose you that job. She had no reason to."

Dave started to protest, but Melissa cut him off. "No more talk about Josie," she insisted, suddenly concerned by Dave's anger. She scooped up a handful of snow and playfully shoved it into Dave's face.

He cried out, startled. Then laughing, he lunged toward her, wrapped his arms around her waist, and tackled her to the ground.

"Let go! Let go! Stop!" Melissa cried, laughing.

They were wrestling in the snow when they heard the crash.

The unmistakable sound of shattering glass.

Melissa climbed to her knees. Raising her eyes toward the school building, she saw Jenkman, staring up at the second floor classroom window that had just been smashed. Even from so far away, Melissa could see the satisfied grin on Jenkman's face.

He must have broken the window with a well-aimed snowball, Melissa realized.

Suddenly a head poked out through the large jagged hole in the window. Melissa recognized Mrs. Powers, the Spanish teacher. "Who threw that?" Mrs. Powers shouted down angrily.

"Not me!" Jenkman called up to her, shrugging, a wide grin on his face. He turned and began to walk away, taking long, loping strides, snickering to himself.

He passed by Melissa and Dave without seeming to see them. He was still chuckling about the smashed window.

"Jenkman's another candidate for your anti-Josie club. He's scary," Melissa said to Dave in a low voice, watching Jenkman walk through the middle of the snowball fight that was still going on down by the street. "He's like a bomb about to explode."

Dave had an unusually thoughtful expression on his face. "Who *isn't?*" he asked with surprising bitterness.

Josie glanced at the grandfather clock in the hallway as she entered the house. A little before six. She shivered as she stamped the snow off her boots. She pulled off her backpack and jacket and tossed the jacket over the banister.

"Muggy! Oh, there you are!" she called as the white terrier came bouncing down the stairs, whimpering with glee. Josie scooped him up in her arms and allowed him to lick her face frantically.

"Hey, you're tickling me!" she cried, laughing.

The lights were all on upstairs. Erica and Rachel must be up in Rachel's room, she figured. "Hey, Mom, are you home yet?" Josie called.

No reply.

Her mother worked such long hours at the phone company. And her father was always on the road, checking on one of his chain of hardware stores. Josie sighed, realizing she hadn't seen him for four days. And with the heavy snow everywhere, he probably wouldn't get home that night.

Josie hugged herself, unable to cast off the chill from being outside. The intercom speaker on the hallway wall crackled. Josie could hear Rachel's voice through the crackling. She seemed to be laughing about something.

There were intercoms all over the house in case Rachel, up in her room where she spent most of her time, wanted or needed anything.

Josie knew the intercom was useful. Necessary, even. But it gave her the creeps. All that crackling. All the voices, so distant yet so near. As if there were ghosts. Invisible lives being lived deep inside the house.

Rachel is a ghost now, she thought and shivered. Such a cold thought.

Should I go up to see her?

Maybe later.

Josie carried her backpack into the den. She clicked on the light and dumped the backpack on the desk.

The den was warmer than the rest of the house. The radiator against the back wall rattled and steamed. Normally, Josie found it a comforting sound. But now the rattling sounded to her like bones tapping against the wall.

Standing beside the desk, she started to unzip the backpack. Just then Luke burst into the den, his eyes wide behind his glasses, his slender face red with anger.

"Oh, hi. You're here," Josie greeted him coldly.

"I'm here and you *weren't*," he said sharply, not trying to cover his anger.

"Give me a break," Josie muttered, turning her attention back to the backpack. The zipper was stuck. She forced it, trying again.

"How could you do that to Erica?" Luke demanded. "How could you make her miss her tryout? Do you know how upset she is?"

"I'll bet you're going to tell me," Josie said.

Her sarcasm made him even angrier. She looked up at him and saw his face turn scarlet, saw the blood pulsing at his temples.

"Then when you do come home, you don't go upstairs," Luke said, narrowing his eyes accusingly. "You don't even check on Erica or Rachel. You're so selfish . . ." His words caught in his throat.

"Listen, Luke—" Josie started.

"That tryout meant so much to Erica," Luke continued angrily. "This is supposed to be an exciting year for her. But thanks to you, she's missing out on everything. She—"

"I'm sorry," Josie said, unable to conceal her impatience. "But that's enough lecturing, okay?" She shook her head, frowning. "Really, Luke. You're not my father. What happens in this house is none of your business."

Luke took a few steps into the den, balling and unballing his fists. He glared at Josie, too angry to speak.

Enough of this, Josie thought, feeling her own anger

begin to rise. I don't need any more lectures from this skinny creep.

"What's your problem anyway?" she cried, the words bursting out. She slammed the backpack against the desk, knocking a silver letter opener to the floor.

"My problem?" Luke's expression remained frozen.

"Why are you still hanging around, Luke? What do you think you're doing here day after day? Why don't you get a life?"

The hurt on Luke's face told Josie that she had gone too far. Stung by her words, he stepped toward her, hands clenched into tight fists at his side.

"Let's just calm down," she suggested, raising a hand as if signaling for a truce.

It was too late for a truce, Josie saw. Luke was too angry.

"You ruined Rachel's life!" he screamed. "Now you're trying to ruin Erica's. You're so selfish, Josie! So unbelievably selfish!"

Something inside Josie snapped. "I haven't ruined *anybody's* life!" she screamed. "I haven't! You know what your problem is, Luke? It's real simple. You're a loser. You're a total loser. You come here every day, acting so good, so superior, pretending to be such a hero, so much better than everyone else. But you're just hiding. You're hiding behind Rachel because you're too big a loser to face the real world!"

The words exploded from her. And when she finished, she was panting noisily for breath, her chest heaving, her hands gripping the edge of the desk as if she were holding on for dear life.

With a single cry of fury, Luke lunged at her. In a quick motion he bent and picked up the silver letter opener from the floor.

"Luke, please! *No!*" Josie screamed.

Chapter 6

EVERYONE'S MAD

Josie stumbled backward until she hit the wall.

Luke stopped short.

His eyes widened in surprise, as if he was startled by what he was about to do.

Josie raised both arms, trying to shield herself from the attack. "Luke, *please!*"

"Noooooooo!" he screamed.

With a loud cry, Luke swung his arm down, digging the blade of the letter opener deep into the top of the mahogany desk.

Breathing hard, he let go of the handle and stepped back. He stared for a long moment at the letter opener standing upright in the middle of the desk.

"Josie," he uttered in a hoarse, frightening voice. "Josie. Almost."

He took another step back, still gasping for breath, his features twisted in horror at what he had just done.

"I've got to get out of here," he said, more to himself than to Josie, his voice barely a trembling whisper.

He ran from the room, bumping the door frame hard with his shoulder but not stopping. Josie stood pressed up against the wall, staring at the letter opener, until she heard the front door slam behind Luke.

Then she exhaled loudly and moved to the desk.

"Wow," she said and cleared her throat, which felt tight and dry. "Wow."

The intercom on the den wall crackled to life. "Josie, are you there? Are you home?" It was Erica from upstairs.

Josie reached for the handle of the letter opener and tugged. "Yeah. I'm home," she called to the small box.

"You're late," Erica said.

More lectures, Josie thought, rolling her eyes. She managed to pull the blade out of the desk top on the second try. She slid some books over to cover the hole.

"Can you come upstairs?" Erica asked. "Rachel is asking for you."

"Maybe later," Josie replied. She had to sit down. She was trembling all over. She had to think. She was terribly shaken by Luke's wild attack.

So out of control, she thought. I've never seen anyone that out of control.

"Rachel wants to see you," Erica insisted, her voice sounding shrill and tinny through the speaker.

"Tell her I'll be up as soon as I can," Josie said irritably.

The intercom clicked off.

Everyone's mad, Josie thought. Everyone's mad at *me*.

And what have I done?

Nothing.

I just want to be left alone.

Still feeling shaky, she moved toward the leather couch. But something caught her eye on the table against the far wall. The day's mail.

She turned and made her way to the table. Sifting impatiently through the magazines and mail-order catalogs, she pulled out a square envelope addressed to her.

Another valentine.

Her breath caught in her throat.

Her hands trembled as she tore the envelope open.

This card was heart shaped. Bright pink. It said, "Hi, Valentine, remember me?" on the front in fancy script.

"Oh, brother," Josie muttered aloud.

Reluctantly she opened the card to find the printed message crossed out and a new message printed beneath it, this time in red ballpoint ink.

> This Valentine's Day
> No memories to save.
> The only flowers for you
> Will be on your grave.

Slamming the card onto the table, Josie glanced up at the calendar on the wall above the desk.

Valentine's Day was Saturday.

This has *got* to be a joke, she thought, forcing herself to start breathing again.

No one is *really* planning to kill me. That's impossible.

Isn't it?

Chapter 7

"I HATE JOSIE!"

The crackling of the intercom woke Josie.

She groaned and squinted at her clock radio. Twelve-thirty at night.

She buried her face in the warm pillow and closed her eyes. The crackling from the box on the wall continued.

Why do we *have* to have an intercom in every room? Josie wondered.

"Josie, please come." Rachel's voice sounded high and frightened through the little speaker.

With a loud groan, Josie pulled herself up, kicking back the covers.

"Josie, come to my room," Rachel said, pleading.

"Why me?" Josie grumbled aloud.

Why is Rachel awake at twelve-thirty at night? And why on earth is she calling me?

The intercom crackled loudly. "Josie?" Rachel's voice sounded strained and scared.

Josie sighed and stretched. "Okay, okay. I'm coming," she muttered.

She lowered her feet to the floor and stood up. It was cold in the room. The old windows rattled from the stiff breeze outside. Her radiator was silent. Outside the bedroom window she could see only solid blackness.

"Josie? Are you coming?" Rachel's voice was a pleading whisper now. Josie could barely hear it over the static.

She made her way through the darkness to the hallway. The floorboards creaked with every step.

I hate this old house, Josie thought. I hate the creepy sounds it makes. The groans. The creaks. This house moans as if it were alive.

Josie shuddered, suddenly afraid.

The kids at school told such frightening stories about Fear Street. About ghosts and evil spirits. About murders and disappearances.

Most of it probably wasn't true. But some of it was.

Fear Street certainly hasn't been lucky for us, she thought bitterly.

Rachel's room was at the far end of the hall. Josie dragged one hand along the wall as she made her way through the dark, creaking hallway. The wall felt cold. Unnaturally cold.

A cold breeze ruffled her nightshirt.

Where was it coming from? she wondered. There were no windows in the hallway.

A ghost's cold breath. The words popped into her mind, causing her to shiver again.

Don't get carried away, she scolded herself.

The floor was cold through the thin carpeting. She jogged past the bathroom, past the guest room. The house groaned and sighed, as if warning her, telling her to go back to bed.

Rachel's room was dark and silent. The door was half-open.

Josie pushed it open all the way and slipped inside, breathing hard. She was chilled and frightened. "Rachel?" she whispered.

No reply.

The room was so dark, she could barely make out the outline of the bed.

"Rachel? Did you call me?" Josie's voice came out a frightened whisper.

No reply.

Josie crept up close to the bed. Closer.

"Ow!" She stubbed her toe against the leg of the bed.

"Rachel?"

Josie could hear her twin's soft breathing. Steady. Slow.

She squinted into the darkness.

Rachel was asleep. On her side. Head resting on the pillow, her long hair loose. A smile on her face.

"Rachel? Did you call me?" Josie whispered.

Rachel didn't stir.

What's going on? Josie wondered, shivering. Did she call me, then fall back to sleep? Did I dream that the intercom came on?

Wrapping her arms around herself, she took a last, lingering look at her sleeping twin. She looks so peaceful, Josie thought. So happy. So *normal*.

She hurried out of the room, tiptoeing silently. She half-walked, half-ran through the cold blackness, holding her breath until she safely got back to her room.

Sliding into bed, Josie pulled the covers up to her chin and shut her eyes.

I've *got* to get to sleep, she thought. I've got two exams tomorrow.

Her heart pounded in her chest. She opened her eyes and stared wide-eyed at the dark ceiling. The light fixture over the bed seemed to be reaching down for her, reaching to grab her.

Again she scolded herself for having too much imagination.

Why doesn't the heat come on? she wondered. Why does it have to be so cold in here? Why can't I fall back to sleep?

She had just started to feel drowsy again when the intercom crackled to life. Josie sat up with a start, listening to the loud static.

"Josie, please come." She could barely hear Rachel's voice over the crackling.

"Huh? What's going on?" Josie cried aloud.

"Josie. Please. Hurry." Rachel sounded strange. Frightened. Her voice very tight.

Josie quickly made her way past the buzzing intercom, out into the hall, the floorboards groaning with each step.

Her bare feet padded over the thin carpet as she hurried down the narrow hallway.

"Rachel? What's wrong?" She stopped in Rachel's

doorway, her heart pounding, and pressed her hands against the door frame to steady herself and catch her breath. "Rachel?"

No reply.

"Rachel? Why'd you call me?"

Silence.

Josie moved silently to the bed. Rachel still hadn't moved. She was sound asleep, on her side, the same faint smile on her face. Her eyes were closed, her breathing gentle and slow.

Josie lowered her face to her sister's. "Rachel?" she whispered. "Are you playing a joke on me?"

Rachel didn't stir.

Josie stared at her for a long time, squinting in the darkness, waiting for a sign that Rachel was really awake, that she was only pretending to be asleep.

Rachel was definitely asleep.

What's going on? Josie wondered as she turned and crept from the room. *What is going on?*

She felt frightened and confused.

She hadn't dreamed the voice on the intercom, the pleading whisper over the crackling static. The voice had been real. Rachel's voice.

Had Rachel been talking in her sleep? She had never done that before.

Was Rachel playing a mean joke? She had never done that before either.

What is going on?

Josie thought of running downstairs to her parents' bedroom and waking her mother. But she decided against it. Mrs. McClain was such a sound sleeper.

She was impossible to wake. Besides, she had to get up so early to go to work. Josie decided not to disturb her.

Instead, Josie returned to her room and dived into the safety of her bed, shivering as she pulled the covers up high. She shut her eyes tight and tried to concentrate on getting to sleep.

But what was that sound?

Was the intercom still on?

Was that someone breathing?

Was that soft laughter she heard?

"Ow. You're brushing too hard."

"Sorry," Erica muttered. She pulled the brush through Rachel's hair with long, gentle strokes. "I was thinking about something else."

"I like when you brush my hair," Rachel said, smiling. She sat in the chair in front of her dressing table mirror, watching Erica's reflection.

Erica stood behind Rachel, raising the brush to the crown of Rachel's head and pulling it all the way down through the beautiful, thick hair, then raising it again, lifting the hair with her free hand as she brushed.

Erica frowned, thinking angry thoughts about Josie. Josie had promised to take care of Rachel this afternoon. She had sworn she wouldn't forget or duck out this time. So Erica had arranged with Mr. Peters to hold a special tryout for her after school.

But after last period, Josie was nowhere to be found. She had completely disappeared. Erica had called home from the pay phone outside the gym, hoping that Josie had gone home. No answer.

Josie had obviously slipped out, forgetting about Rachel once again. She was probably somewhere with Steve.

Erica had no choice but to apologize to Mr. Peters and hurry home to wait for Rachel. She had spent the last fifteen minutes brushing Rachel's hair, thinking about what she would say to Josie, growing angrier with every brush stroke.

"Is Josie coming to see me?" Rachel asked suddenly.

It's as if she was reading my mind, Erica thought, startled. "No, Josie isn't home right now," she told her sister.

"Brush harder," Rachel said, staring up at Erica's reflection in the rectangular mirror.

"Okay." We need to have a family meeting, Erica thought angrily. I can't let Josie do this day after day.

"I was very smart in school today," Rachel said, grinning like a little girl.

"That's good," Erica replied distractedly.

"The teacher said I was very smart," Rachel said.

"That's very good," Erica told her, pulling the brush through the straight red hair.

Rachel's expression turned thoughtful. "Josie is my sister, right?" she asked, wrinkling her forehead in concentration.

"Yes," Erica replied. "Josie is your sister. Your *twin* sister."

Rachel thought about this for a long while. Then she

surprised Erica by saying, "Josie doesn't like me anymore."

"No!" Erica protested, letting the brush slip out of her hand. She bent down to pick it up from the carpet. "Josie still likes you, Rachel. Why would you say such a terrible thing?"

"No. Josie doesn't like me. Josie doesn't talk to me."

"That's not true—" Erica started, but Rachel interrupted.

"Well, I don't like Josie anymore!" Rachel cried, her green eyes lighting up. "I *hate* Josie!"

"Rachel, calm down!" Erica scolded, putting a firm hand on Rachel's trembling shoulder. "Calm down. Don't get all excited."

"I *hate* Josie!" Rachel repeated. "I hate her. I hate her. I hate her."

"Don't say that," Erica insisted. "Shhh. Just calm down. Let's brush your hair some more. Okay?"

The phone rang.

Erica tossed the brush onto the dressing table and hurried to her room to answer it.

"I hate Josie! I hate Josie!" she could hear Rachel chanting.

"Rachel, please!" Erica shouted, reaching for the phone. She raised the receiver to her ear. "Hello?"

"Oh, hi. Is this Erica?" a boy's voice asked.

"Yes. Hi."

"It's me. Jenkman."

"Oh, hi, Jerry," Erica said enthusiastically, revealing how pleased she was to hear from him.

"Is Josie there?" Jenkman asked.

Erica's enthusiasm faded. For a moment she had thought Jenkman was calling to talk to *her*.

"No. Josie isn't home," she told him dispiritedly. "I don't know where she is."

"Oh," Jenkman said, sounding very disappointed. Then, to Erica's shock, he added, "Did Josie get my valentines?"

Chapter 8

MATH PROBLEMS

"Dave, you look terrible," Melissa said earlier that same Thursday at school.

"Thanks for the pep talk," Dave muttered, shaking his head.

They lingered outside the door to Mr. Millen's classroom. Dave was leaning against the tile wall, his black hair scragglier than usual, his dark eyes red rimmed, ringed with dark half circles.

"I didn't get much sleep last night," Dave said, scratching his jaw. "This math exam. I'm really sweating it."

Melissa *tsk-tsked* sympathetically.

"Hey, how's it going, Kinley?" Donald Metcalf gave Dave a hearty punch on the shoulder as he headed into Millen's classroom. "You going to ace this test?"

"Yeah. I'll ace it if I don't copy off you!" Dave replied, rubbing his shoulder. "Metcalf is really a big ox," he whispered to Melissa.

"You're in a *great* mood," Melissa said sarcastically. "Metcalf is your buddy, remember? From the wrestling team?"

"I'm sorry I talked my parents out of getting me that math tutor," Dave confessed, changing the subject back to the exam. "I really thought I could get this stuff. But I don't understand it. I missed three days with the flu, and I've never caught up." He yawned noisily and shifted his backpack on his shoulder.

The bell rang right over their heads, startling them both.

Josie McClain hurried past them into the room, diving into her seat as the bell stopped ringing.

"You'll do okay," Melissa told Dave softly, putting a reassuring hand on his shoulder.

"No, I'm dead meat," he said forlornly. "Dead meat."

"Millen's tests are never that bad," Melissa assured him. She tugged affectionately at a scraggly strand of black hair that had fallen over his forehead. "Come on. Let's go in before Millen starts to howl."

She grabbed the sleeve of his sweater and pulled him into the room. Dave slumped into his seat behind Josie. Melissa continued on down the front row and took her seat in the corner.

Mr. Millen began passing test papers back down the rows without saying a word. A few seconds later he gave the okay to start.

The room was silent, so silent Melissa could hear the buzzing of a fluorescent light on the ceiling above her head. Melissa read over the entire test. There didn't appear to be any surprises. She dived into the first problem, scribbling calculations on lined paper, referring back to the test paper as she worked.

She was halfway through the fourth problem when she saw Josie walk up to Mr. Millen. Josie leaned down to speak to the teacher, who was slouched at his desk, poring over a magazine.

The teacher glanced up, startled. Josie began to whisper close to his ear.

From her seat in the front row, Melissa could hear Josie's whispered words clearly. "Mr. Millen, would it be okay if I move my seat?" she asked.

"Move? Why?" Mr. Millen stared at her suspiciously.

"Well . . ." Josie whispered reluctantly, glancing toward the back of the room. "Dave Kinley is copying off my paper."

Melissa could feel her face grow hot.

Dave is in big trouble now, she thought unhappily. I can't believe Josie is doing this.

Josie and Mr. Millen whispered a bit longer. Melissa strained but couldn't make out any more words. She saw Josie gather up her test and scrap paper and move to an empty seat by the window.

Melissa wondered if Dave knew he was in trouble. She returned to her test, struggling to concentrate.

Why didn't Dave ask me to help him with this stuff? she wondered.

Too proud, she decided.

Sometimes Dave was just plain weird. He never liked to let on that he had a problem, that he was human. He always liked to pretend that he was on top of things, that he had everything under control.

At least he could have asked me to study with him, Melissa thought, shaking her head.

Now what's going to happen?

She didn't have to wait long to find out.

When the bell rang ending the period, the test papers were passed to the front. Mr. Millen collected them all, then dismissed the class.

"Oh, Dave, could you see me for a minute?" he called, his face expressionless.

Melissa saw Dave hesitate at his desk. "S-sure," he stammered.

Melissa closed her eyes. Poor Dave, she thought. He's dead meat, just as he predicted.

She gave him a worried glance as she passed him and headed out the door. She stopped across from the classroom, greeted a few friends who were passing by, then leaned against the wall to wait for Dave.

He appeared a few minutes later, his face bright red, his expression glum. "Josie turned me in," he muttered and uttered a few curses.

Her head bowed sympathetically, Melissa began walking toward her locker. Dave followed, muttering angrily.

"Can you believe it?" he demanded. "Can you believe that little rat would do that to me?"

Melissa stopped at her locker and raised her eyes to his. "But did you do it, Dave? Did you copy off her paper?"

"So what if I did?" Dave snarled.

Melissa dropped back, startled by his anger.

"Are you going to get on my case too?" he cried.

"I just asked," Melissa replied softly. She unsnapped her combination lock and pulled open her locker. "So what did Millen say?"

"That big jerk? He said he was giving me a zero," Dave told her, his voice breaking. "That test counts for half the grade. So I get a zero for half my grade." He kicked a locker angrily. "You know what that means? It means I get kicked off the wrestling team."

"Oh no!" Melissa cried.

"Yeah, I get kicked off the wrestling team," Dave repeated bitterly. He cursed some more. "And that means I don't get my wrestling scholarship. And that means I can't go to college. All because of that—"

At that exact moment Josie came walking by.

Dave reached out and grabbed her arm.

"Ow!" she cried. Her eyes flashed at him. "Let go of me!" she screamed nastily.

"Why'd you do it?" Dave demanded, squeezing her arm.

"Let *go* of me!" she repeated shrilly. She jerked her arm out of his grasp.

"Why'd you turn me in?" Dave insisted, his dark eyes wide with fury.

"I don't want to talk about it," Josie said coldly, glancing past him to Melissa. "I mean, what choice did I have? You were leaning over so far to see the answers, you were breathing on my neck!"

Dave sputtered in rage but no words came out.

Josie spun away and hurried around the corner. Several kids had stopped to stare at the angry confrontation.

Dave uttered an angry cry and slammed Melissa's locker door shut, the sound echoing down the hall.

"She's wrecking my life!" he screamed at the top of his lungs. "I *hate* Josie McClain!"

"Dave, stop! You're totally losing it!" Melissa cried.

He didn't seem to hear her. With another angry cry, he took off after Josie.

"Dave, come back!" Melissa screamed, terrified by his rage. "Come back! What are you going to do?"

Chapter 9

FIRST BLOOD

*J*osie stared at the social studies textbook. The words became a blur, shimmering black streams on the white page.

She'd been gazing at the same page for half an hour, unable to concentrate. She couldn't get Dave Kinley out of her mind.

I can't believe he and I used to go together, she told herself.

She thought of their angry confrontation in the hallway at school. All because she had told Mr. Millen that he was cheating. She didn't want to get Dave in trouble, but what choice did she have? There he was, practically hanging over her shoulder, copying every answer. He was bound to get them both in trouble. And that wasn't fair. She had studied hard for that test.

I did the right thing, Josie decided. So Dave is

angry. Big deal. Dave is always angry about something. He'll get over it.

She returned to her social studies book, but the words refused to come into focus. Feeling nervous, upset, she pushed her chair back from the desk and started to pace back and forth.

The clock said it was seven-thirty. Josie still had a lot of homework to do.

I'm so tired, she realized. I didn't get much sleep last night. Because of that intercom.

Because of Rachel. Calling me. Calling me again and again.

Asleep all the while.

A shiver crept down Josie's back.

She glanced at the rectangular gray box on the wall, and as she looked at it, it clicked on. She heard a cough, then Rachel's soft, pleading voice. "Josie, can you come to my room?"

"No!" Josie shouted, startled by her own outcry. "No! Not again! Not again!"

"Josie, please come to my room," Rachel's voice pleaded softly from the small speaker.

"No!" Josie cried. "Erica is there, Rachel. Erica will take care of you."

I've got to get out of here, she decided. I can't take this tonight. I really can't!

She grabbed her blue down jacket from her bed and hurried out of the room. The intercom speaker buzzed and crackled. Rachel's pleading voice seemed to follow Josie down the stairs.

She didn't breathe until she was outside. She

slammed the door behind her. At last Rachel's voice disappeared.

Was Rachel really calling me?

Was it a trick?

Am I cracking up?

Josie didn't care. She just had to get away. Away from all the anger. Away from all the pain.

It was a clear, cold night. The snow crunched under her feet as she made her way to the car in the driveway. Her breath steamed up, gray against the black night sky.

Somewhere down the block a cat cried, sounding like a human baby.

Steve, Josie thought. I'll go see Steve. He's the only one who understands.

"This was a good idea," Josie said, flashing Steve a warm smile. "I was so upset. But now I feel calm." She grabbed his gloved hand and pulled him along with her.

"You're a good skater," Steve said, struggling to catch up to her.

Josie's skates glided almost silently over the ice. She loved to skate, sliding so fast, feeling so weightless and free. She let go of Steve's hand and, moving gracefully, started around the circular rink.

There were only a few other people at the Shadyside Indoor Rink, a couple of younger kids stumbling over each other with their mother cheering them on, and another teenage couple, dressed in bulky sweaters and wool ski caps, not from Shadyside High.

Josie completed her circuit, gliding effortlessly,

enjoying the slicing sound her skates made on the ice. "Watch this," Steve said, grinning. He started skating backward.

"Not bad," Josie told him, grinning. She skated up to him as he backed around the rink, smiling at her.

"Can you do this?" he asked, challenging her.

"I don't think so," Josie admitted. "You know who's the *really* good skater in my family? Erica. She's not at all athletic. But she can really skate."

"Next time I'll invite *her!*" Steve joked.

Thinking of Erica made Josie think of Rachel. Her smile faded. She shook her head hard as if trying to shake away her thoughts.

"Can we sit down for a bit?" she called to Steve.

Seeing the change in her expression, he agreed.

A few minutes later they were sitting in a corner of the small skating rink café, sipping steaming hot chocolate from white cardboard cups.

"Thursday's a good night to come here," Steve said, glancing around the cavernous building. "There's no one here. It's almost like having our own private rink."

Scooting his chair in, he accidentally banged the tiny metal table with his knee, causing a little of Josie's hot chocolate to spill over the side of the cup. "Sorry," he apologized. "That was klutzy."

"I don't care," Josie said, distracted. "Coming here was a great idea. A real life saver. I just had to get out of the house."

He locked his eyes on hers. His smile faded. "Things are tough at home?"

"It's just so depressing," Josie said, her voice catching in her throat. "I-I'm just so unhappy at home. All the time."

She took a sip of the hot chocolate. It burned the roof of her mouth, but she didn't care. She could feel her unhappiness welling up, about to burst out of her.

Should she hold it in?

No. She couldn't hold it in any longer.

She had to talk to someone. Steve was a good listener.

Steve squeezed her hand. "You're depressed because of Rachel?"

Josie nodded. "Because of Rachel. Because of Erica. Because of everyone."

"What's going on?" Steve asked, nervously tapping the metal tabletop with his fingers.

Josie told him about the night before, about the intercom clicking on, about Rachel calling to her in that tiny, whispery voice, then appearing to be asleep.

"I—I feel so guilty about Rachel," Josie continued. "Every time I see Rachel I feel guilty. Every time I see that sweet smile, that childish expression. Every time I brush her hair. Every time I talk to her. Every time I realize that Rachel will always be like a child, that Rachel will never grow up. Never have a family. Never have a real life. Every time I see her, so beautiful, so—helpless. It just makes me want to cry, Steve. I feel so guilty. So helpless too."

Steve exhaled loudly, shaking his head. "I don't know what to say," he muttered. "I guess it'll just take time. I mean—"

"Erica makes it even worse," Josie interrupted. "All

Erica does is *try* to make me feel guilty. Guilty about not spending time with Rachel. Guilty about not spending more time with her. Guilty about not taking care of Rachel. But I just can't *bear* it, Steve. Why can't Erica give me some space? I mean, she *must* realize that I feel guilty enough already."

"Don't upset yourself," Steve said uncomfortably. "Want to skate some more?"

Josie shook her head. She could feel hot tears form in the corners of her eyes, but she didn't care. She let them run down her cheeks without attempting to wipe them away.

"I still love Rachel," she said. "She's my twin sister, after all. I love her, but I can't stand to be with her, to see what's happened to her. That's why I stay away as much as I can. That's why I only go home when I absolutely have to."

"It'll get better," Steve said lamely. "You'll see." He finished his hot chocolate. Then he tapped the bottom of the cup nervously against the tabletop. "Really. You'll see, Josie."

She shook her head and wiped her wet cheeks with both hands. "Erica doesn't understand," she continued, ignoring Steve's discomfort. "She thinks I'm just being mean. Irresponsible. But I'm not. She just doesn't understand. *Nobody* does."

"Josie, really—" Steve started.

"Look," she interrupted. She reached into the back pocket of her jeans. "Look at this one."

She unfolded a card. Another valentine. A bouquet of red roses on the front. She shoved the card at Steve with a trembling hand. "Just look at this one."

He took the card and read the handwritten rhyme aloud in a sing-song voice.

> "Who's sending these cards?
> Don't bother to wonder.
> On Valentine's Day
> You'll be six feet under."

Steve stared at the rhyme, printed carefully in black ink. He narrowed his blue eyes thoughtfully. "Do you still think Jenkman's sending them?" he asked.

"Ever since I dumped him, he's been following me around, pestering me like some kind of sick psycho."

"These have to be jokes," Steve said, closing the card and handing it back to Josie. "Just stupid jokes."

Josie crumpled the card into a ball and shoved it into her nearly empty hot chocolate cup. "You think so?"

"Jenkman is weird, but he's not a murderer!" Steve declared. "It's just a stupid joke, Josie. You shouldn't take it seriously."

"I—I don't know *how* to take it," Josie stammered. "This is the third one. They're really starting to get me scared. What if he *means* it?"

"Call him up and tell him to stop it," Steve advised. "It's just his dumb way of getting back at you for not going out with him."

"He's impossible," Josie said. "He follows me home from school. He's always at my locker. He calls sometimes and—"

She stopped abruptly. Her mouth dropped open. She pointed over Steve's shoulder toward the ice. "Steve!"

Steve caught the alarm in her eyes. "What's the matter?" He scooted his chair back and turned around to follow her gaze.

"There's someone there," Josie told him, her voice revealing her fear. "Someone is watching us. From behind the food stand."

Steve stared hard. "I don't see anyone."

Josie jumped to her feet, knocking her chair over. It clattered noisily to the concrete floor. "There!"

"I see a shadow," Steve said, "but—"

"Is it Jenkman?" Josie asked.

"I don't know." Steve stood up too. He stepped around the table and grabbed Josie's arm. "Do you want to go?"

She nodded. "Yes, let's get out of here. Please!"

They returned their skates and hurried out the door.

As they stepped out into a cold, clear night, Steve pulled her close and kissed her. She leaned against the skating rink doorway and kissed him back. She raised her hands behind his head. His blond hair felt surprisingly soft. She held his head tightly, pulling him to her, forcing him to continue the kiss.

She realized she didn't want the kiss to end. She wanted to stay there like that forever. In the clean, cold wind. In the silent darkness. Alone with Steve.

She didn't want to think about who was spying on her inside the skating rink. She didn't want to think about the scary, threatening valentines.

Most of all she didn't want to go home.

A short while later she found herself saying good night to Steve in her driveway. The old house, bathed in an eerie yellow glow from the porch light, hovered in front of her, cold and uninviting.

Josie leaned across the front seat of the car for one last good night kiss. Then, sighing, she pushed open the car door and reluctantly headed up to the front porch. She waved to Steve, pulled the front door closed behind her, and stepped into the dark front hallway. She could see the twin headlights of Steve's car roll down the wall as he backed down the drive.

"Anyone awake?" Josie called in a half-whisper.

It wasn't that late, she knew. Around eleven o'clock.

She tip-toed past the intercom on the wall as if not wanting to awaken it. She could see a light on in the kitchen.

"Who's here?" she asked, making her way quickly toward the kitchen. "Erica? Are you up?"

She took a few steps into the kitchen and stopped. No one there.

Who left the light on? she wondered.

There were some bowls beside the sink. Someone must have had ice cream, Josie decided.

She took a few more steps. Stopped again.

There was something sticky on the bottom of her sneaker.

Had she stepped in gum or something?

She leaned down to examine her sneaker.

And saw what she had stepped in. A dark red puddle.

Cranberry juice? Had someone spilled cranberry juice? And not wiped it up?

No. There was too much of it.

Another puddle.

And another dark puddle, even larger.

Josie followed the trail of puddles with her eyes across the linoleum to the kitchen door, which led to the backyard.

Why was the door open?

Staring in horror at the figure lying in the doorway, Josie knew at once what the dark puddles were.

She raised her hands to her face and started to scream.

SOMEONE IS HAPPY

Chapter 10

SOMEONE IS HAPPY

Staring in horror at the blood-soaked figure sprawled on the floor beside the open kitchen door, Josie screamed.

She shut her eyes, but the hideous sight remained with her.

"Muggy!" she cried. "Oh, Muggy!"

Opening her eyes, she took a reluctant step toward the unmoving animal.

"Muggy. Muggy," she wailed.

The little terrier was on its back, its head twisted to the side, eyes wide in a blank, unseeing stare.

The wind battered against the glass storm door, startling Josie. She grabbed the Formica countertop for support as her entire body lurched in a tremor of horror.

Josie felt sick. She started to turn away, but something caught her eye.

What was that shiny thing in Muggy's stomach?

Pressing both hands over her mouth, she squinted at it. It took her a while to realize it was a letter opener. A silver letter opener. The letter opener from the desk in the den.

"Who did this?" she cried out loud, hot tears streaming down her cheeks.

Her horror was rapidly turning to anger. *"Who* did this?"

How had it happened? Had someone come to the back door? Had Muggy come running to investigate?

Josie tried to picture it. Someone pulled open the storm door, came into the kitchen, and murdered the poor little dog with the letter opener from the den.

But who? Why?

"Muggy," Josie cried, shutting her eyes again, shutting them so tightly they hurt. "Oh, Muggy."

Josie suddenly realized she wasn't alone in the kitchen.

Opening her eyes, her hands still pressed against her face, she turned to find Rachel standing right behind her.

Rachel wore a long blue-flannel nightdress. Her hair was tied back and fell forward over one shoulder. She looked very pale in the fluorescent light of the kitchen.

Rachel's emerald eyes were aglow as she stared at

Muggy's corpse, and Josie was horrified by the evil smile on her twin's face.

"Rachel!" Josie cried, turning to face her.

"There's the puppy," Rachel said brightly, her smile growing wider. Rachel pointed down to the gruesome sight. "There's the puppy."

Why is she so happy? Josie asked herself, suddenly frightened. Why does she think this is funny?

"There's the puppy," Rachel repeated in her singsong voice.

"Rachel, you shouldn't be down here," Josie scolded, still gripping the top of the counter.

"But there's the puppy," Rachel insisted, smiling, her green eyes shiny and excited.

Without warning, Erica appeared behind Rachel. "When did you get home?" she asked Josie. And then her eyes fell on the murdered dog. "Oh no!" Erica cried weakly. Her mouth dropped open in horror.

"There's the puppy," Rachel said, pointing.

Rachel's words seemed to break Erica out of her silent spell.

"Oh, no," she muttered. "Oh no, no, no, no." Then Erica's expression changed. She grabbed Rachel's shoulders, her features tight with concern. "Come away, Rachel. Come with me."

"But there's the puppy," Rachel protested.

"Don't get upset, dear," Erica told Rachel sternly. "Don't get upset. Come upstairs." She dragged the still-smiling Rachel out of the kitchen.

Josie, left alone, shut her eyes once again. Why

was Rachel so happy? she asked herself, suddenly feeling exhausted and drained. Why was Rachel so happy?

And who came into my house and murdered my dog?

Chapter 11

"SOMEBODY HATES YOU"

Melissa pushed back the curtains from her bedroom window and stared out into the night. The sky hovered low and purple, dotted with pale white stars. The trees in the front yard appeared to shiver from the cold.

Across the street the McClains' house was dark except for the yellow porch light. Melissa had been at her window a few minutes before, at a little after eleven. She had seen Steve's car pull up the drive. She had seen Josie get out of the car and walk slowly up to her house.

Josie's spending all her time with Steve these days, Melissa realized. And as little time as possible at home.

It must be hard for her, Melissa thought, surprised to be feeling any sympathy for Josie.

Earlier in the evening Melissa had walked across the street and paid a visit to Erica and Rachel. Erica had been glad to see her. Rachel seemed preoccupied. She hadn't even acknowledged that Melissa was there.

Even during the short visit, it was easy for Melissa to pick up on Erica's growing resentment and unhappiness. She was spending more and more time with Rachel because Josie was seldom home.

If only the McClains could afford full-time help for Rachel. They had a nurse who came on weekends. That was all they could afford, Erica had unhappily explained. Mr. McClain's hardware stores were struggling, and times were tough. Mrs. McClain worked long hours, but her salary barely paid the household expenses.

After the visit Melissa had returned home. She had called Dave, but his mother said he'd gone out. She had no idea where.

Melissa spent the rest of the night doing a little studying and a *lot* of pacing back and forth and staring out the bedroom window.

She pulled the curtains back into place, glanced at the clock radio—nearly eleven-thirty—and decided to see if Dave had returned home.

He picked up on the second ring.

"Where've you been?" Melissa demanded, not intending to sound so shrill.

"Huh? Nowhere," Dave replied, surprised by her burst of anger.

"I called you before. Your mom said you went out," Melissa said, softening her tone. She stood in front of her dresser mirror as she talked, toying with her sleek, black hair, pushing strands off her forehead, tugging at strands on the sides. "I was over visiting Rachel. Then

I came home and called you. I—I was worried about you."

"Well, I'm *terrible,"* Dave said glumly. "I've been cruising around all night. Just driving. I couldn't even tell you where I went. I'm so deranged."

"You're always deranged," Melissa teased, trying to cheer him up.

"Ha-ha," he said bitterly. "Coach kicked me off the wrestling team after school today," Dave said softly, so soft Melissa could barely hear him.

"Huh?"

"You heard me. I'm definitely off the team. Because of Josie."

"Oh no!" Melissa exclaimed. "When you said it before I didn't really think he'd kick you off."

"There goes my wrestling scholarship. There goes college. There goes my whole life," Dave moaned.

"Don't exaggerate," Melissa scolded.

"All because of Josie," Dave said bitterly, ignoring her.

"You shouldn't blame Josie," Melissa said softly.

"Why not?" Dave demanded angrily. "Why shouldn't I blame her?"

"She didn't cheat on the math test," Melissa said.

Dave uttered a low curse. "Josie's messed up my life. I hate her. I really do."

"Don't talk like that," Melissa said, turning away from the mirror and shutting her eyes. "You frighten me when you talk like that. You really do."

"I don't feel like talking now," Dave said abruptly. "Bye." He hung up without giving her a chance to reply.

"Hey!" Feeling hurt, Melissa stood staring at the phone. She was tempted to call him back. He had no reason to hang up on her like that.

She set the receiver down instead.

Sometimes when Dave got like this, it was best to leave him alone. Let him simmer by himself for a while.

Sighing, she started to get undressed.

What was that flashing red light outside? Flying saucers?

That was Melissa's first thought.

She hurried to the window and immediately saw that the flashing light was atop a black-and-white police car parked in the McClains' driveway.

The McClains' front door was open. The police officers must have gone inside.

What's going on? Melissa wondered. I hope everyone's okay.

A short while later Melissa, her forehead pressed against the cool glass, saw two police officers come walking out. Their faces, caught in the porch light over the McClains' front door, were grim. One of them was shaking his head.

They talked for a short while to Mrs. McClain, who remained in the house, holding open the glass storm door. Then the two officers walked slowly to their squad car, turned off the flashing light, and drove away.

The McClains' porch light went out, casting the rambling old house into total darkness.

Melissa yawned. She was dying to know what had happened, but it was too late to call. She'd have to wait until morning. Anyway, things looked pretty normal.

Yawning again, she tugged the curtains back into place and crossed the room to start getting undressed for bed.

"That one policeman looked sick," Josie said quietly. "You know, the redheaded one. When he saw Muggy, I thought he was going to puke."

"They both acted really grim," Erica agreed.

The two sisters were in their nightshirts, lying on Erica's bed. Erica's head was on her pillow. Josie was stretched out across the foot of the bed.

Mrs. McClain was in Rachel's room. The house was silent now.

Josie ran her hand along Erica's quilted bedspread. She closed her eyes and pictured the hideous scene on the kitchen floor. After the officers left, promising a serious investigation and warning the McClains to lock their doors from now on, Mrs. McClain had tried to clean up. But the blood had soaked into the linoleum, leaving a dark reminder of the murder that had taken place there.

Josie shuddered. "Poor Muggy."

"I can't believe it," Erica said, sitting up and unhooking her long, jangly earrings and setting them down on the bedside table.

"Someone must have come in through the back door," Josie said. "But why? To rob us?"

"Nothing was taken," Erica said, shifting her weight.

"Then whoever it was came in just to kill Muggy," Josie said, thinking out loud. "They knew Muggy was my dog, and . . ."

"We don't know that," Erica said. "We don't know who—or why."

"Didn't you hear anything?" Josie asked almost accusingly. She sat up. "Didn't you hear anything at all? In the backyard or the kitchen? Didn't you hear Muggy barking or anything?"

Erica shook her head thoughtfully, struggling to remember. "Not a sound," she said finally. "Melissa came over for about half an hour . . ."

Josie made a sour face.

"Then I took Rachel up to her room," Erica continued. "I tried to get Rachel to watch television so I could study, but she seemed nervous tonight, edgy. So I read to her for a while, and then—"

"I don't need a minute-by-minute account of your thrilling night," Josie snapped impatiently.

"Well, I didn't hear a sound. Mom went grocery shopping. She got back a little after eight-thirty. I remember hearing her talking to Muggy when she put the groceries away. And I remember her yelling at Muggy to stop barking when she was talking to Daddy on the phone. That was at about nine-thirty, I guess."

"I know who did it," Josie said bitterly, lost in her own thoughts, barely hearing a word of Erica's. Her eyes watered over. She blinked several times, then wiped her eyes with the sleeve of her nightshirt. "Jenkman."

"Huh?" Erica pushed herself upright.

"Jenkman," Josie repeated, her eyes brimming with tears. "That creep. He wanted to hurt me. I'll bet he murdered Muggy to scare me and make me think the threats he's been sending are going to come true."

"It wasn't Jenkman," Erica told her sister, speaking softly but firmly.

Josie turned and stared hard at Erica, studying her face. "It wasn't? What makes you so sure?"

"I just know it wasn't Jenkman," Erica replied with surprising defensiveness. "For one thing, Jenkman didn't send those threatening valentines."

"How do you know that?" Josie demanded suspiciously.

"He told me," Erica explained. "He sent those other ones you got. The two funny ones. The ones signed 'Secret Admirer.'"

"You talked to Jenkman?" Josie asked, her eyes wide with surprise. "When? What about?"

"The other day. He called to talk to you," Erica said. And then she added with obvious bitterness, "But, of course, you weren't here. Of course, you were out."

"So?" Josie asked impatiently.

Erica sighed. "So I told him about the ugly threatening cards. He swore he didn't send them. He told me he only sent those two funny cards."

Josie climbed to her feet and crossed her arms over her chest. She glared at Erica. "And you believed him?"

"Yes," Erica insisted shrilly. "He's not a liar, Josie."

Josie uttered a bitter laugh. "Since when are *you* an

expert on Jenkman?" she demanded. "You know, Erica, I think you have a crush on that creep. Look at you. You're blushing."

Erica turned away. "What if I do?" she said angrily. She swallowed hard. "It doesn't matter. Jenkman doesn't know I exist. I'm just someone to take phone messages for you."

"He's a creep," Josie said, making her way to the window and peering out. The light was still on in Melissa's room across the street. "He's a creep and he's dangerous. And he hates me." She shuddered and stepped back from the window.

"He doesn't hate you," Erica told her. "He's still sending you valentines, still calling you, still trying to get your attention."

"Yeah. Get my attention. By killing my dog," Josie said, her voice catching in her throat. Tears formed in her eyes again. This time she let them run down her cheeks.

"Josie, listen—" Erica started.

"I should call the police back," Josie interrupted her. "I should tell them to go question Jenkman."

"It wasn't Jenkman," Erica insisted softly. "I think it was Luke."

Her accusation stunned Josie. Josie froze in place, then slowly shook her head. "No, no way," she said. "Luke has a temper. But he's basically a wimp."

"Luke is very angry at you," Erica said.

"Tell me something I don't know," Josie sneered, rolling her eyes. "But he's basically a wimp, Erica. He wouldn't kill Muggy."

Erica started to reply, but their mother appeared in

the doorway just then, a worried expression on her face. "Josie, would you go brush Rachel's hair for a bit?"

Josie glanced at the clock on Erica's wall. "But, Mom, it's after midnight," she protested.

"I know," Mrs. McClain said, sighing wearily. "But Rachel is very upset. About Muggy, I'm sure. She's very tense, very excited, Josie. I can't get her to go to sleep. Would you help me out? Just go in and talk soothingly to Rachel and brush her hair for a while."

"Sure, Mom," Josie replied, shaking her head unhappily. She brushed past her mother and made her way down the hall to Rachel's room.

Rachel was in her nightdress, sitting in the big, overstuffed armchair across from her bed, her hands in her lap. Josie stopped in the doorway to stare at her twin.

She looks so pretty, so childlike, Josie thought. The light from the floor lamp behind the chair illuminated Rachel's hair from behind, giving it a coppery glow. Like a halo, Josie thought. Rachel was like a pale, pretty angel.

"Hi, Rachel. Would you like me to brush your hair?" Josie asked softly. She stepped into the room and picked up the hairbrush from the dresser.

Rachel didn't reply. Her expression was thoughtful, and she seemed to be staring off into the distance.

"It's very late," Josie said. She stepped behind Rachel, tenderly pulled her long hair back over the armchair, and started to brush it.

As she brushed, she saw a smile form on Rachel's

face in the mirror on the far wall. "You like to have your hair brushed, don't you," Josie said, yawning.

Rachel's smile grew wider. "Somebody hates you, Josie," she whispered.

"Huh?" Josie wasn't sure she had heard correctly. "What did you say, Rachel?"

"Somebody hates you," Rachel repeated a little louder. She giggled. "Somebody really hates you."

Josie lowered the hairbrush to her side. She moved around the chair and stared at the gleeful grin on Rachel's face. "Rachel, do you know more than you're letting on?" Josie asked. "*Do* you?"

Rachel stared straight ahead, her smile mysterious. She giggled again. "Somebody hates you," she said teasingly, turning her green eyes on Josie.

Staring back at her smiling twin, Josie felt a stab of cold fear.

Chapter 12

MAYBE JENKMAN

*A*fter school on Friday afternoon, Josie slammed her locker shut. After brushing her hair out of her eyes, she pulled her wallet from the back compartment of her backpack and started to count her money.

"Where you going?"

Josie saw Erica standing beside her, ready to brave the snow, her wool muffler wrapped several times around the collar of her winter coat.

"I'm going to that new card shop," Josie told her, shoving her wallet back into the backpack and lifting the heavy bag onto her shoulder. "You know. It's called Greetings. It opened next to The Corner. I've got to buy a valentine for Steve. Tomorrow is Valentine's Day, and I'll bet all the good ones are already gone."

"Can I come with you?" Erica asked somewhat forlornly.

"Yeah, sure," Josie replied, zipping up her down jacket.

"Mom is home today to take care of Rachel," Erica said, "so we have plenty of time."

"You have any money?" Josie asked, leading the way to the front doors. "I'm down to about three dollars."

"I think I have a five," Erica replied. "But you have to promise to pay me back."

"Promise."

They headed out of the school into the gray afternoon. The snow had become hard and icy. Patches of dark ground were showing through. A cold wind gusted and swooped around them, cutting one direction, then the other.

Erica buried her face under her wool muffler. Josie pulled her blue and white ski cap lower and leaned into the wind as they turned up Park Drive, walking quickly.

"I got my math exam back," she told Erica. "I got a ninety-two."

"That's great," Erica said from under the muffler. "I have so much homework, I'm going to be up all night."

"Poor thing," Josie replied with mock sympathy. Then she shrieked in fright at the loud burst of sound just behind her.

I've been shot! she thought.

Her breath caught in her throat. Her heart seemed to stop.

"Josie, are you okay?" Erica asked, startled by her

sister's terrified reaction. "It was just a car backfiring." She turned and gestured toward an old Chevy station wagon that had rumbled past.

Josie let her breath out slowly. She forced a laugh. "Oh. Sorry. I-I'm just so nervous ever since . . ." Her voice trailed off.

"You got white as a sheet," Erica exclaimed, shaking her head. "Did you think it was a gunshot?"

Josie nodded. "I've been so jumpy and sad since Muggy was killed last night. Every little noise makes me jump. All I think about are the threats in those cards and Muggy."

Erica said something in reply, but her words were drowned out by the roar of a large moving van speeding by. After it passed, the sisters crossed the street and entered the new card shop.

Josie paused in the doorway. It was a long, narrow store with two aisles that ran between stainless-steel shelves loaded nearly to the ceiling with cards. A young woman with close-cropped blond hair sat behind a cash register at the front, a bored expression on her rather plain face. There were several other customers in the store, most of them pawing through the valentines, pulling them out one by one, reading them silently, putting them back in their slots.

Josie turned to the front shelf. She pulled off her red wool gloves, shoved them into her coat pockets, and began examining cards.

"There's more in the back," the woman at the register called to her. "Those have pretty well been cleaned out."

"Thanks," Josie said distractedly. She was reading a

really crude, insulting card. Making a disgusted face, she quickly returned it to the shelf.

Why do people want to insult each other on Valentine's Day? she wondered. Of all days!

Why do people want to kill people on Valentine's Day?

The question crashed uninvited into her mind.

Meanwhile Erica made her way through the narrow, crowded aisle to the back of the shop. An enormous valentine, nearly the size of a wall poster, caught her eye, and she stopped to read the cornball rhyme in it.

When she looked up, she was startled to see Jenkman at the end of her aisle.

He didn't see her at first. He was concentrating on pulling out valentines and examining them. Erica stared at him, waiting for him to recognize her. He was wearing a brown leather bomber jacket and black jeans.

"Hey, Jenkman!" she called finally.

He turned toward her and his face turned bright red. He shoved the cards he'd been holding back on to the shelf. "Oh, uh, hi," he said, obviously very embarrassed.

He walked rapidly up to Erica, peering over her shoulder as he approached.

He didn't want me to see the cards he'd selected, Erica thought. He's so embarrassed. It's as if I caught him committing a crime or something.

"Hi, Erica," Jenkman said, still gazing beyond her. "Just buying some cards for my mom."

"That's nice," Erica told him, giving him a warm smile. "I was—"

"Is Josie here?" he interrupted. "Oh, yeah. There she is." He hurried past Erica, pushing her aside with both hands to get down the narrow aisle. "Hey, Josie! Hi! Josie!" he shouted.

He never even glanced at me, Erica thought unhappily. She followed him down the aisle, eager to see how Josie would react.

At first Josie pretended she didn't hear Jenkman calling to her. But when he was only a few feet away, she turned and glared at him coldly.

"Josie—" he started.

"Did your mother let you out of your cage?" she asked, turning up her nose.

"Josie, listen," he pleaded, grabbing her arm.

She jerked back as if he had hit her.

"I just want to talk to you," he said, stung.

"Buying more ugly valentines for me, Jenkman?" she asked. "Going to scrawl more ugly threats?"

"Huh?" His face filled with confusion. Then he seemed to remember. "Hey, Erica told me about those cards, Josie. You don't think that I sent them, do you?"

"Three guesses," she said coldly. "And were you spying on me the other night? At the skating rink?"

"No way," Jenkman said heatedly. "Why would I spy on you?"

"I don't believe you," Josie told him. "Why don't you get a life?"

"I don't get you," Jenkman said.

"That's right. You *don't!*" Josie snapped. "Bye, Jenkman."

Before he could say anything else, she hurried out of the store.

Embarrassed, Erica made her way quickly to the second aisle and started toward the exit. She turned at the doorway.

Jenkman, she saw, had returned to the card rack in the back. His face was bright red, his expression angry. He was furiously pulling card after card off the rack without reading them, without even looking at them.

He looks angry enough to kill, Erica thought.

Maybe he *is* the one who's sending Josie those valentines.

Maybe it *is* Jenkman after all.

Chapter 13

VALENTINE'S DAY

Steve leaned forward and kissed Josie. She kissed him back. His lips were hot and dry. He smelled of peppermint.

"Happy you-know," he said, grinning, his breath steaming up in front of him.

"Is that all I get? One lousy kiss? No valentines? No chocolates?" Josie teased, pressing both hands against his chest.

"What was so lousy about the kiss?" he demanded.

Josie laughed. "Come inside. It's freezing out here. Brrr." She shivered.

He followed her into her house.

"I'm so tired of winter," she complained, rubbing her arms. "You'd better have a Valentine's Day present for me, mister."

"I might," Steve teased.

She led him into the living room. Luke, in a heavy,

old-fashioned-looking gray overcoat, was coming the other way. "Oh, hi, Steve."

"Hi, Luke. How's it going?" Steve asked, pulling off his jacket and tossing it onto the couch.

Luke shrugged. "Not great. I—uh—brought Rachel a big Valentine's Day heart. You know. Chocolates. But she just stared at it."

"Oh," Steve said awkwardly.

Luke pushed his glasses up on his nose. "Rachel seems very troubled tonight," he said, turning to Josie. "Something's bothering her. Of course, she doesn't say what." He took a deep breath. "Well, I've got to get going."

"Yeah. Well. See you," Steve said.

Josie and Steve watched Luke head out the front door. When it closed behind him, Steve turned to her. He scratched his jaw. "I can't decide about Luke," he said.

Through the living room window, Josie watched Luke climb into his car in the driveway. "What do you mean?" she asked.

"Well, I can't decide if Luke is a great guy for sticking with Rachel. Or if there's something wrong with him."

Josie sighed impatiently. "Come on. It's Valentine's Day. Let's not talk about Rachel tonight, okay?"

"Okay," he agreed. He leaned down to kiss her, but she shoved him away.

"No present. No kiss."

"You're tough," he teased, grinning. "Hey, are we going ice-skating, or not?"

"I don't know," Josie said reluctantly.

"You said that's what you wanted to do," Steve protested, disappointed. "We had so much fun the other night."

"Yeah. Till I came home and found my dog murdered," Josie muttered. She raised her eyes to him. "I'm kind of scared."

"You mean—"

"I mean, it's Valentine's Day, the day I'm supposed to die. Here. Look." Josie walked rapidly to the den. She reappeared a few seconds later carrying another valentine.

She jammed it into his hand. "Here. Read this— the latest one." Her eyes locked onto his, revealing her fear.

Steve was surprised by her fear. Then, frowning, he opened the card. He read it aloud:

> "Roses are black,
> Violets are gray.
> On Valentine's Day,
> You'll start to decay."

Steve stared at the handwritten message for a long while. "Do you recognize the handwriting?"

Josie shook her head. She took the card from him and folded it between her hands. "Maybe we shouldn't go out," she said softly.

"It's a stupid joke," Steve replied, frowning. "It's just dumb. We shouldn't let it spoil the whole night." He took her hand, surprised to find it ice-cold. "Come on, Josie. I told Dave Metcalf and Cory Brooks and some other kids we'd meet them at the ice-skating rink."

Josie pulled her hand from his. "I really don't think we should go out tonight," she insisted. "The stupid valentines are probably a joke, but what if they're not? What if someone is really crazy enough to . . ." Her voice trailed off. She tossed the card down on the couch. "Let's rent a video and stay here."

"But we had such a great time the other night," Steve protested.

He started to say more, but the intercom on the wall clicked on.

They heard crackling sounds, then someone breathing.

Then Rachel's voice, whispery, soft, and teasing. "Someone hates you, Josie," Rachel said. "Someone really hates you."

Josie uttered an exasperated cry. She grabbed the sleeve of Steve's sweater. "Let's get out of here!" she cried and started to pull him toward the front door.

"Somebody hates you, Josie," Rachel repeated over the intercom in a whispery, sing-song voice. "Somebody hates you."

Steve grabbed his jacket. "We're going ice-skating?"

"I don't care where we go," Josie replied, pulling her jacket from the front closet. "I just have to get *out* of here! Rachel gives me the *creeps* lately!"

Tossing her jacket over her shoulder, she started to pull open the front door. She turned to see Steve hanging back.

She followed his glance. He was staring at the folded-up valentine on the couch cushion.

"Josie, somebody hates you a lot!" Rachel's voice came over the intercom.

"Steve, I have to get out of here!" Josie cried. "I

can't take this. I really can't." She motioned for him to hurry.

As Steve made his way to the door, a new voice came on the small speaker on the wall. It was Erica's, and she sounded upset. "Josie, are you going out? The nurse had to leave early and I'm here alone."

"Yes, I am going out. See you later!" Josie called impatiently into the box.

"But how *can* you?" Erica demanded unhappily.

"What difference is it to you? *You* don't have a date tonight," Josie said cruelly. Then she added, "I'll take care of Rachel tomorrow. Promise."

"I don't believe you," Erica said angrily, her voice making the small speaker vibrate. "Listen, Josie—"

"Bye, I'm gone," Josie said brusquely and stepped out the front door. Steve followed, a troubled expression on his face, and pulled the front door shut behind him.

It was a cold, clear night. Most of the snow had melted. Small patches stood up on the front lawn like icebergs in a dark ocean.

The bare trees were still as if frozen in place. A pale half moon was high in the charcoal sky. Josie gazed up but couldn't see any stars. Somewhere down the block a dog howled mournfully.

Their sneakers squished on the wet ground as they made their way down the lawn to Steve's car at the curb. Holding on to Steve's arm, Josie glanced at Melissa's house across the street. All the lights were on. She could see someone's shadow behind the drawn shade in an upstairs room.

At the curb she pulled open the car door, started to

lower herself to the seat, then stopped. "Steve, look," she said, motioning back to the driveway.

Steve turned to follow her gaze.

"It's Luke," Josie said, lowering her voice to a whisper.

Luke's car was still in the driveway up near the house. In the yellow light from the porch, Josie could see Luke sitting behind the wheel. He seemed to be staring straight ahead, not moving.

"What's his problem?" Steve asked, leaning against the car door as he stared at Luke's car.

"I don't know," Josie replied, bewildered. "Why is he just sitting there?"

"Think I should go talk to him or something?" Steve suggested.

Josie shook her head. "No. I don't know. I mean, he's okay, I think. Maybe he just wants to be alone or something."

"Weird," Steve said, shaking his head. He lowered himself into the car.

As they drove down Fear Street, heading toward town, Josie was surprised to find herself becoming more and more frightened.

She tried to force them away, but the upsetting images of the past week invaded her mind. Muggy dead. The dark puddle of blood. Rachel's giggling response. Rachel so gleeful as she announced that somebody hated Josie. The valentines. The horrible valentines with their scrawled, ugly threats.

She stared out into the passing night, dark yards and houses whirring by, and felt the waves of fear roll over her body. "Steve," she said softly, touching his arm as if making sure he was real and not just another image. "Steve, maybe we should turn back."

"You'll be okay," he said soothingly. "Really."

"But those valentines. They all said I'd die today."

"A stupid joke, Josie," he replied calmly. "A horrible, stupid joke. Don't worry."

"But I *am* worried," Josie admitted in a trembling voice. "I'm very worried. . . ."

112

Chapter 14

ERICA IS WORRIED

*E*rica squinted through the darkness to the clock on her bedroom wall: 2:03.

She pulled herself up in bed and lowered her feet to the floor.

Staring at the clock, she stretched and listened to the silence.

The house was dark and still.

I'm the only one awake, Erica told herself unhappily.

Her father was still away on his business trip. Her mother had returned from a party at the neighbors' house at about eleven-thirty and had gone right to bed.

Mom is sleeping peacefully, Erica thought. She's such a sound sleeper, she doesn't know. She doesn't know that it's after two in the morning and Josie isn't home.

I'm the only one who's awake.

With a groan, she stood up and untwisted her nightshirt. Then she made her way across the dark room to her desk, the floorboards creaking under the thin carpet.

She clicked on the desk lamp, blinking as her eyes adjusted to the bright white light. Leaning on the edge of the desk, she reached for the phone directory.

She dropped the directory on the desk, then flipped quickly through the *B*'s until she found Barron. Steve's phone number had been underlined in red ink, probably by Josie.

Keeping her finger on the number, Erica glanced up at the clock. She sighed and punched Steve's number, leaning against the old oak desk as she waited for the ring.

"Hello?" Steve answered halfway through the third ring, his voice hoarse with sleep.

"Steve?" Erica whispered.

"Uh-huh. Who's this?"

Erica started to reply, then heard a loud *clunk*.

"Sorry," Steve said after a few seconds. "Dropped the phone."

"Were you asleep? It's Erica."

"Huh? Erica?" Steve said the name as if he'd never heard it before. "Yeah. I was asleep. I . . . uh . . ."

"Steve, I'm so worried," Erica told him, her voice revealing her fear. "Josie isn't home."

The line was silent for a long moment. "Not home?" Steve finally replied, sounding alert. "What time is it?"

114

"It's after two," Erica told him.

"It is?" He sounded very surprised. "But Josie should've been home hours ago."

"I don't understand," Erica said, starting to sound more than a little frantic. "Wasn't she with you? Didn't you bring her home?"

"We had a fight," Steve replied, speaking rapidly in a low, steady voice.

"You *what?*"

"We had a stupid argument," Steve repeated. "It was really dumb. About skates or something. I don't even remember what started it."

"And what happened?" Erica asked, lowering herself into her desk chair. Her hand gripped the receiver so tightly, it began to ache.

"Well, Josie left," he told her reluctantly.

"By *herself?*" Erica cried in alarm.

"No, huh-uh," Steve answered quickly, sounding very defensive. "She left with a whole bunch of kids."

He cleared his throat loudly, then continued. "We were all at the rink together. After we had that dumb argument, Josie left with them. With the others." He cleared his throat again. "But—but she should have been home hours ago, Erica."

"I know," Erica said unhappily.

"Do you think—?" Steve started.

"Oh. Wait!" Erica interrupted. "That's the front doorbell. That must be Josie. Bye."

Erica hung up the receiver without waiting for Steve's reply. Then she hurriedly padded down the front stairs in the darkness, her bare feet making the stairway groan and creak.

Eagerly, she turned the lock and, using both hands, pulled open the front door.

"Josie?" she cried.

Chapter 15

TERRIBLE TROUBLE

*E*rica uttered a silent gasp.

She blinked, trying to force her eyes to adjust to the harsh yellow porch light.

It wasn't Josie.

Standing grim faced on the other side of the glass storm door were two dark-uniformed police officers.

Erica recognized them immediately. They were the same men, the young-looking redhead and the older one, bald in front with a wide salt-and-pepper mustache, who had come to their house after Muggy had been killed.

They gazed in at her, their features set, their eyes narrowed.

Erica pushed open the storm door with a trembling hand. "Is—everything okay?" she asked haltingly.

She could tell by their expressions that everything *wasn't* okay.

"Are your mother and father home?" the older one asked somberly.

"My dad is away," Erica told him, her voice trembling. "But I can call my mom."

Suddenly chilled, she held the glass door open for them. The two police officers stepped inside quickly, silently. They seemed to bring the cold in with them. To Erica the room temperature dived to below zero.

The older one pulled the storm door shut. His partner removed his cap and nervously scratched his curly red hair.

Erica turned and was startled to see her mother already behind her in the hall. Mrs. McClain was struggling to tie the belt of her robe with trembling hands.

"Erica?" she asked, her voice still choked with sleep. "What's going on?"

"I'm afraid I have some very bad news," the older police officer said softly.

Mrs. McClain gasped and reached out to grab the banister with her right hand to steady herself. "About Josie? Where is she? She isn't home?"

Erica shook her head no and shut her eyes.

"There's no other way to say this but to say it," the officer said in a low steady voice. He took a deep breath. "Mrs. McClain, your daughter has been murdered."

Mrs. McClain uttered a shrill shriek. Her knees buckled and she collapsed onto the floor of the hall.

"Noooooooooo!" As she landed, she let out a piercing wail that sounded more animal than human.

The two officers lunged forward to help her. She

landed hard, straight down on her knees, still wailing. "Not Josie. Please—*not Josie.*"

"How did it happen? How do you know? How do you know it's Josie?" The questions poured out of Erica in a desperate voice she didn't recognize. "Who did it? How do you know? What if—"

The red-haired officer helped the sobbing Mrs. McClain to her feet. "Not Josie. *Please,* not Josie!" she kept repeating, enormous tears running down her quivering cheeks.

"We found your sister in the alley behind the ice rink," the older police officer told Erica, speaking in a low, professional voice. "We identified her by her wallet. She hadn't been robbed. She was dead when we arrived. She had been stabbed in the back. With the blade of an ice skate. The skate was still in her back."

"Ohhhhh." Erica moaned. She stared wide-eyed at the grim-faced man for a long while. Then her eyes rolled up in her head. Her knees bent, and she crumpled in a heap to the floor.

The older officer bent quickly to help her.

"No! No! Please—no!" Mrs. McClain was still screaming.

"Ma'am, do you have a family doctor?" the red-haired officer asked, holding on to her shoulder. "Perhaps the doctor could come out and—"

He stopped in midsentence, startled as another figure floated down the stairway. Rachel emerged from the shadows, wearing a long, flowing white nightgown, her hair down over her shoulders.

"Somebody hates Josie," Rachel declared in a

bright sing-song voice. She had an eerie smile on her face. "Somebody really hates you, Josie."

Still leaning over the unconscious Erica, the older policeman's expression darkened. "What? What did you say?" he called suspiciously up to Rachel.

"Somebody hates Josie," Rachel repeated, smiling, her green eyes sparkling in the hall light.

"Huh?" The two officers glanced quizzically at each other.

"Ignore poor Rachel," Mrs. McClain told them through her tears, shaking her head sadly. "Just ignore her. She doesn't know what she's saying."

The next morning, Sunday morning, Melissa had planned to sleep late. But she was startled awake by her mother's voice, calling from downstairs.

"Melissa, phone!"

"Huh?" Melissa muttered, slowly raising her head from the warmth of her pillow.

"Phone, Melissa!"

Melissa pulled herself up and rubbed her eyes. She struggled to focus on the clock radio. Only eight-thirty.

"Hey, Mom, why'd you wake me?" she shouted irritably. "Why didn't you tell them to call back?"

"It's Dave," Mrs. Davis shouted patiently. "I wouldn't have awakened you, but he said it was important."

Dave?

What could Dave possibly want at eight-thirty on a Sunday morning?

This better be good, Melissa thought, yawning.

She picked up the phone extension on her bedside table. "Hello? Dave?"

"Hi, Melissa. I . . . uh . . ."

"Dave, what's the matter?" Melissa asked with concern. "You don't sound good."

"Melissa, I've got to talk to you. Right away," Dave said breathlessly. "I-I'm in terrible trouble."

Chapter 16
A STUPID THING

Melissa pulled on jeans and a sweater and hurried to The Corner, the small coffee shop near Shadyside High.

Dave was already in a booth in the back when she arrived. He was wearing a faded, blue-denim work shirt with the collar turned up. He was tapping the tabletop nervously with a blade from his Swiss army knife.

He looked up as Melissa slid in across from him, but didn't smile. His small, dark eyes were red rimmed and tired looking, Melissa noticed. His long, black hair was unbrushed.

"Hi," she said tentatively. "You look terrible! Did you hear about Josie?"

He folded up the knife and set it down on the white Formica tabletop. He nodded. "Yeah, I just heard it on the news."

122

"I can't *believe* it!" Melissa exclaimed. "I mean, I just saw Josie on Friday. And now, this morning . . ."

The waitress, a short young woman with frizzy orange hair, stepped up to the table and set down two water glasses. "You need menus?"

They shook their heads and ordered omelets and fries.

"It's so horrible," Melissa continued after the waitress had walked away. "I haven't been to their house yet, but my mom called over there, and they're all in shock."

Dave shook his head, but didn't say anything. He slid the red-handled knife back and forth across the table from hand to hand. They sat in silence for a while.

"I mean, *murdered,*" Melissa said, shuddering at the thought of it. "It can't be." She took a sip of water.

Dave remained silent, continuing to slide the knife, his eyes on the table.

Melissa sighed. "I heard the police are questioning Steve," she said.

"That's what I have to talk to you about," Dave said with sudden urgency. He closed his left hand over the knife and held it in place on the table.

"Huh?" Melissa stared at him, bewildered.

"I don't know how to say it," Dave said uncomfortably, his dark eyes burning into hers.

"You—you know something about the murder?" Melissa stammered.

"Listen to me," Dave said heatedly. "Just listen. I did a stupid thing. A very stupid thing." He stopped to take a deep breath.

"Dave," Melissa started reluctantly. "Did you—"

"Who gets the one with extra cheese?" the waitress interrupted, balancing the tray of dishes on her hip.

As the waitress set the omelets and fries down, talking all the while, Melissa stared across the table at Dave. She felt a heavy dread moving up from the pit of her stomach.

What was Dave starting to tell her?

He looked so guilty. So frightened.

How horrible was the secret he was about to reveal?

The waitress finally finished and, slapping the tray against the side of her uniform, headed up toward the front.

Dave stared down at his food but didn't begin to eat it. His eyes darted nervously around the small restaurant, as if making sure no one was listening.

"Dave, what were you trying to tell me?" Melissa asked.

The smell of the grease was starting to make her feel sick.

Or was it the tension?

Dave cleared his throat nervously. "I did a really stupid thing," he repeated, avoiding her stare. "I sent Josie some valentines."

Melissa's mouth dropped open. *Is that all?* she asked herself, feeling a little relieved.

"Valentines? To Josie?" she asked, her high-pitched voice revealing surprise. "But what's the big deal?"

"You don't get it," Dave said, frowning. Melissa saw that beads of perspiration had broken out across his forehead. "I sent her special valentines. It was so stupid, I can't believe I did it."

124

"I *knew* you were still hung up on her," Melissa said, allowing some anger to creep into her voice.

"No—wait—I wrote things on the valentines I sent to her," Dave confessed, blushing.

"What kind of things?" Melissa demanded, feeling sick. She shoved the french fries away from under her nose.

"Well . . . uh . . ." Dave hesitated. Then he let it all out in a burst of words. "I wrote rhymes on the cards. I crossed out the words that were there and wrote my own rhymes. I said—I said she was going to die on Valentine's Day."

"Huh?"

Again Dave glanced quickly, nervously, around the restaurant. It was deserted except for an elderly couple having scrambled eggs at the counter.

"It was supposed to be a joke. I was so angry at Josie. I hated her so much," Dave said, struggling to explain, searching for every word, his face still bright red. "I don't know why I did it, really. It was stupid."

Tapping his fingers nervously on the tabletop, he looked away.

Melissa took a deep breath. His words seemed to be swimming around in her mind, bobbing around, not making any sense. "You sent her death threats?" she asked.

"No," Dave answered heatedly. "Well, yes. I mean, not *real* ones. It was a joke. I wasn't serious, but—"

"Is everything okay?" the waitress asked, appearing beside the table once again. "Can I bring you anything else?"

"We—uh—haven't started yet," Melissa told her, glancing down at the untouched food.

"Well, I can't *eat* it for you!" the waitress joked, and headed back toward the kitchen, laughing uproariously.

"So you sent Josie cards saying she was going to die on Valentine's Day?" Melissa asked, still trying to comprehend what had happened. "Did you sign them?"

"No," Dave snapped. "No way. But, don't you see, Melissa? I sent the cards, and then she was killed on Valentine's Day. I—"

"Oh, no!" Melissa gasped. "When the police see the cards, they'll think you killed Josie."

Dave nodded in agreement, but didn't speak.

Staring across the table at him, sick and frightened and confused all at once, Melissa felt a sudden chill, a chill of suspicion.

"Dave," she said, staring hard at him, her voice a low whisper. "Dave, tell me. You didn't kill her, did you?"

Chapter 17

DANGEROUS PLANS

Dave stared back intently at Melissa. He didn't reply.

As she waited for him to say something, she studied his eyes. His eyes, she knew, would reveal the answer more truthfully than his words.

What did she see in them?

Guilt? Anger? Fear?

"I didn't kill Josie," Dave said finally in a flat, exasperated tone. "How can you ask me a question like that?"

"I had to ask," Melissa told him, still searching for the answer in his dark, narrowed eyes.

"Listen, I hated her enough to send the threatening cards," Dave said, leaning over the table and lowering his voice. "But I didn't hate her enough to kill her."

Are you lying? Melissa wondered, studying him. No. No, you're telling the truth—aren't you?

Aren't you?

She wanted so desperately for him to be telling the truth.

"I—I got the idea last winter," Dave started to explain. "When Josie's dad suddenly called and said I couldn't work in his store over Christmas vacation. I knew Josie was behind it. My Christmas was ruined. I was so angry. I wanted to pay her back. I got the idea to send her a Christmas card with some kind of warning on it."

Melissa shook her head. "I don't believe this. You were going out with me, but you were still hung up on Josie." She struggled to keep her jealous feelings down. Josie was dead, even though she couldn't believe it.

"No, no way," Dave insisted. "Don't say I was hung up on Josie. I hated her. Really."

"So you sent a threatening Christmas card?"

"No. I—I didn't get it together to send the Christmas card. I got busy and forgot about it. Then when Josie didn't get off my case, I—I don't know. I guess I just lost it. I sent her two threatening valentines. Then, after the cheating thing happened in math class, I sent more. And now Josie's dead, and my writing is all over the cards, and the police are going to think . . ." His voice trailed off.

Melissa stared down at the food on the table, probably cold by now. Her mind whirred without focusing. She wanted to yell and scream at Dave and tell him how stupid he'd been. But she also wanted to say something helpful, something encouraging.

He was terrified. He needed her help.

But what could she do?

"I just wanted to scare her a little. That's all," Dave said, tapping the fork rapidly against the side of his plate. "It was just a dumb joke."

"Where did you go after you left my house last night?" Melissa asked. "Did you go straight home? Were your parents up? Did they see you?"

Dave shook his head, frowning. "I left your house a little after ten, right? Then I just cruised around for a couple of hours. I guess I was feeling restless. I don't know. I just drove around. I didn't get home till nearly one. My parents were asleep."

"So you have no alibi?" Melissa asked, swallowing hard, her throat dry and tight.

"You're starting to sound like some kind of cop show on TV," Dave snapped.

"I'm just trying to help!" Melissa cried.

Dave poked the omelet with his fork. Some cheese oozed out. He kept tapping the plate, avoiding her stare.

Raising her eyes to the front of the small coffee shop, Melissa saw two kids she knew from school enter. She watched them, hoping they wouldn't take a nearby booth. She breathed a sigh of relief when they took the booth closest to the front window, out of hearing range.

"Hey, what makes you think Josie kept those valentines?" Melissa asked, brightening a bit.

"Huh?" Dave dropped the fork to the table.

"Yeah," Melissa said with growing enthusiasm for the idea. "I bet she threw them out. Why would she keep them? I don't think I'd keep them if *I* got them."

Dave thought about it for a moment. "I'll bet she

showed them to Erica," he said glumly. He put his elbows on the table and cradled his head in his hands. "I'll bet Erica saw them all. She'll tell the police."

"But, Dave—"

"Maybe Erica's already shown them to the police," he muttered. "Maybe the police are already looking for me."

"Erica hasn't talked to the police," Melissa told him. "Erica is in shock or something. I told you my mom called over there this morning. Their doctor answered—he said that Erica and Mrs. McClain both had to have medication. You know, to help them sleep. I guess Erica fainted. Then, when they revived her, she went totally ballistic."

"Then maybe I have a chance," Dave said, picking up his head, his expression thoughtful.

"What do you mean?" Melissa asked. "A chance?"

He didn't answer. She could see that he was thinking hard, concentrating.

"What are you thinking?" she demanded impatiently.

"Maybe I can get the cards back," Dave told her.

"What? How?"

"I'll sneak into the McClains' house and get them."

Melissa stared at him, frowning in disbelief. "Are you crazy? How are you going to get in? What are you going to tell them when they see you pawing through Josie's things? I really don't think—"

"No, no. Wait a minute," Dave said, putting a hand over Melissa's. "I'm not going to do it while they're home."

"But I just *told* you," Melissa insisted. "Erica and her mother are both—"

"The funeral will be tomorrow, right?" Dave interrupted, his dark eyes glowing with excitement.

"Yeah, I guess."

"Well, they'll all be at the funeral," Dave explained. "The house will be empty. I'll sneak into the house, grab the valentines, and get out."

Melissa locked her eyes on his. "Do you really think you can?"

"Sure," Dave assured her. "What could go wrong?"

Chapter 18

"HELLO? ANYONE THERE?"

Dave parked his car at the corner and sat staring down Fear Street, the engine still running.

Even though it was just past eleven in the morning, the sky was black. Large raindrops, one every few seconds, splattered on the windshield. The low, dark clouds promised a heavy storm.

The old oaks and maples and birches that bordered the street bent low, as if cowering from the storm. Their bare branches shivered in the swooping wind.

Dave cut the car engine. He reached for the door handle.

Now or never, he thought.

He took a deep breath and pushed the car door open.

Dead brown leaves swirled at his feet as if trying to push him back into the car. But he stood up, slammed the car door, and hurried quickly toward the tall hedge just beyond the curb.

A large raindrop hit his forehead, and the cold water ran down his nose.

Keeping low against the hedge, he made his way toward the McClains' house in the middle of the block.

This was supposed to be easy, he thought, ducking behind a tall evergreen shrub as a red van slowly passed, its headlights cutting through the morning darkness.

It was supposed to be easy. So why was his heart pounding like a bass drum? And why were his legs so weak he could barely walk?

Another raindrop splattered the shoulder of his leather jacket. He bent low, eyes to the street, and moved past another yard, trying to jog, but slipping on some wet leaves.

He stopped near the McClains' driveway. The house loomed in front of him like a giant, dark creature. Two upstairs windows stared down at him like unfriendly eyes.

No cars in the drive, he saw. No lights on in the house.

They were all at the funeral.

Half of Shadyside was probably at the funeral. Dave thought. Even the school had been closed so that Josie's friends could attend.

Dave turned his gaze across the street. Melissa's house was dark too.

Darkness everywhere.

He took a deep breath and held it, trying to slow his racing heart. Then, shoving his hands deep into his jeans pockets, he leaned forward into the cold wind and made his way quickly up the rain-spattered asphalt drive.

I'll be in and out of there in no time, he told himself. I'll grab the valentines and split. Piece of cake.

He knew he was giving himself a pep talk. He didn't care.

He needed all the encouragement he could get, even if it came from himself.

He was only a few yards from the house now, approaching the flagstone walk that led to the front porch.

A loud crash at the side of the house made him cry out and leap into the air. He spun around, prepared to run.

Then he saw the metal garbage can roll on its side across the driveway.

The wind had toppled it.

"Wow!" He exhaled loudly, shaking his head.

This was supposed to be easy. *Easy!*

The rain started to come down harder. Squinting through the large drops, he examined the house.

A small rectangular basement window at ground level was partway open. If worse came to worst, he figured, he could probably squeeze through it.

But he wanted to try the doors first. Maybe he'd get lucky. Maybe the McClains had left one of them unlocked.

Should he try the front or the back?

He hestitated, a heavy sick feeling in the pit of his stomach. He hadn't eaten any breakfast. He'd been too nervous. Maybe that had been a mistake.

His stomach growled as if warning him away.

Despite the rain and the cold swirling winds, he realized he was sweating. His hands were cold and wet.

Which door—front or back?

Don't just stand here in the driveway waiting for someone to come by and see you! he scolded himself.

He decided to try the front door. He was so close to it, after all.

He climbed the wooden steps. His legs felt as if they weighed a thousand pounds.

What was that sound?

It took him a few seconds to realize it was his own breathing.

He pulled open the storm door. He reached for the brass knob with a trembling hand.

He turned it and pushed.

The door swung open.

I don't believe it! he thought, scrambling inside.

He pushed the door shut behind him and leaned back against it, waiting to catch his breath.

I'm in. I'm inside. Just like that.

The front hallway was dark. Dark as night.

Silent as a tomb.

I'm in. Now what?

He struggled to think clearly. He wished he could turn on a light. He wished his heart would stop pounding.

Got to get upstairs, he told himself. To Josie's room.

Calm. Calm.

There's plenty of time. The funeral is just beginning.

The funeral.

Funeral.

The word sounded so strange.

Stop stalling, he scolded himself. Get upstairs.

He pushed himself away from the doorway.

He took a step in the dark, narrow hallway. Then another.

A grandfather clock ticked noisily.

"Hey—!"

What hit his knee?

Squinting, he saw the wooden umbrella stand.

"Give me a break," he muttered, his voice sounding tiny and hollow in the empty darkness.

He was nearly to the front stairway when he heard the intercom.

Dave stopped right in front of the box on the wall.

Had it just clicked on?

No, it must have been left on.

He moved his ear close to the small round speaker.

Crackling sounds.

Just static. Empty static.

Or *was* it?

Dave listened carefully. Was that *breathing*? Was someone breathing into it?

No.

Yes.

"Hello? Anyone there?" he called into it, bringing his mouth right up to the box.

No reply.

He listened.

He couldn't tell if he heard breathing or just the normal crackling and static.

"Anyone there?" he said again.

Silence.

Exhaling loudly, he made his way up the stairs, each step creaking under his weight. He stepped onto the landing, his hand reluctant to let go of the banister.

It was even darker up there.

He knew which bedroom was Josie's. He had visited her there once when she was sick. Back when they were going together.

The floor groaned beneath him as he walked quickly into her room. Rain drummed noisily against the bedroom window as if trying to break in.

The bed was neatly made, an old teddy bear on the pillow.

As if waiting for Josie to return.

A neatly folded stack of freshly laundered clothes was piled on a chair beside the window.

Dave sighed.

This is definitely creepy he thought. Josie was here two days ago. Now she'll never be here again.

He made his way to the old oak desk in the corner. Leaning over the desk chair, he started to search the desk top with both hands.

"Got to find the cards and get out of here," he said out loud, his voice a trembling whisper.

A strong gust of wind made the old windows rattle. The entire house seemed to shudder in reply.

I *hate* these old houses, he thought, feeling his panic rise, choking him.

I hate Fear Street and I hate these old houses. I hate the rain and I hate the wind and I hate—

"Where *are* they?" he asked himself aloud.

He pushed aside a stack of school papers.

He searched through another pile of notebooks and binders.

No, not here.

But they *have* to be here. They *have* to be.

A wave of nausea swept over him. He stopped searching. Swallowed hard.

Where *are* they?

Not on the desk.

Of course they're not. She would never keep them out. She probably shoved them into a drawer.

He grabbed the drawer handle. Pulled so hard he almost pulled the entire drawer out of the desk.

Calm down. Calm down. He repeated the words over and over, but it didn't seem to help.

Where are they? Where *are* they?

He riffled frantically through the contents of the drawer.

No, not here.

Then where?

Where?

He shoved the drawer back into the desk, his hands trembling. His breath coming in loud gasps.

He dropped down onto his knees and peered under the bed.

Nothing there but dust.

What was that sound?

A car?

A car door slamming?

"I've got to get out," he muttered out loud, in a shrill, quivering voice he didn't recognize. "Out. Got to get out."

He'd failed.

He coulnd't find them.

Now someone was coming. He had to get out and fast!

His heart pounding, he climbed to his feet and lurched to the doorway. In the dark, narrow landing, he turned toward the stairs.

Halfway to the stairs, he stopped short.

And cried out in shock and horror.

Chapter 19

ANOTHER VICTIM

Swirling reds.

Puddles and pools.

Blood red.

Shimmering and rolling, spinning around him.

And behind the angry spills of color, Dave's scream, a hideous animal wail.

Of horror.

Of anger.

The scream refused to fade.

The red pools refused to disappear.

The scream continued to echo until it was replaced by new sounds.

A rumble at first.

Thunder?

No. Too close to be thunder.

And too human.

Footsteps, Dave realized.

The rumble and creak of footsteps on the stairs.

Heavy footsteps, moving closer. Rapidly moving closer.

The two officers ran up the stairs and burst into the hallway.

One of them reached for the light switch. The overhead light clicked on, a white sunburst, an explosion of light.

"Hey, you—!"

The two officers moved quickly across the landing. One of them reached for his pistol.

"Drop it!" the other one yelled to Dave.

Dave stared at the blood-covered letter opener gripped so tightly in his hand.

The red flowing onto the silver.

"Drop it! Now!" the policeman barked.

Dave leaned over the girl. He stared at the bloody wound in her side. Stared at the puddle of blood at his feet.

Erica.

The girl was Erica.

He huddled over Erica, staring at the stab wound.

The blood red swirls floated angrily in Dave's eyes. Blinding him.

Suffocating him.

So much blood.

Poor Erica.

Such a big, red wound. And so much blood.

Puddles and pools.

Such an angry, angry red.

Why was Erica here?

Why were the police here?

Why wouldn't the red pools go away?

Dave whirled around. He started to stand up.

"Stop right there, son," the officer said, tensing the arm that held the pistol aimed at Dave. "Drop the knife and don't move. You're in a lot of trouble."

PART TWO

FEBRUARY, ONE YEAR LATER

Chapter 20

MELISSA'S TURN

Melissa leaned forward to kiss Luke and bumped her forehead against his glasses.

"Ow!" they both said.

Melissa gave Luke a playful shove with both hands. "Don't you ever take those glasses off?" she chided.

He laughed and pulled his glasses off. He gazed at her expectantly, waiting for another kiss. But Melissa surprised him by jumping to her feet.

"Hey, come back," he called. "What's wrong?"

Melissa walked to the den window and stared out at the darkening sky. Gray clouds collided over the bare trees, threatening a snowstorm. By the side of the garage, two large crows were pecking at the hard ground. Melissa watched them till they flew away, squabbling loudly.

"I got a letter from Dave," she told Luke, still staring out the window, her arms crossed over the front of her pale green sweater. She uncrossed her arms and began to fiddle with a tangle of black hair.

"Huh? From Dave?" Luke reacted with surprise.

Luke and Melissa had been going out for about two months. In all that time, she had mentioned Dave only once or twice. Dave, Luke knew, was in some military-style boarding school upstate. Luke wasn't exactly sure where.

"Poor Dave," Melissa said, turning to face Luke, sitting against the windowsill. "He really lost it."

"Yeah," Luke agreed thoughtfully, putting his glasses back on.

"He always had a terrible temper," Melissa said, still toying with her hair. "But I never thought he killed Josie and stabbed Erica. I still don't believe it."

"I can't believe it happened a year ago," Luke said softly. "It—it's all so fresh in my mind."

"I still have nightmares about it," Melissa confessed. "Getting the letter from Dave brought it all back."

Leaning against the windowsill, feeling the chill from outside against her back, the frightening events of one year before whirred rapidly, painfully through Melissa's mind.

Dave had been caught huddling over Erica's unconscious body, the blood-soaked letter opener in his hand. Erica was rushed to the hospital where she eventually recovered. Dave was arrested and held.

But the police investigation couldn't link Dave to Josie's murder. And Erica never pressed charges, never accused him of stabbing her. "It was too dark," she had told the police. "And I was attacked from behind. I never saw who did it."

Why had Erica been home?

She had been in a state of shock, too sick and upset to go to Josie's funeral. She had stayed home with Rachel while her parents went to the funeral.

She heard strange noises over the intercom. She called the police. She stepped out into the dark hallway to investigate—and was stabbed from behind.

Dave told the police that he hadn't been the one who stabbed Erica. He claimed that he had stumbled over Erica's body while trying to get to the stairway. She had already been stabbed. Dave was so shocked and horrified, he bent down and picked up the letter opener.

He froze there in a panic. That was when the police came up the stairs and found him.

Dave swore he was innocent, and after a long investigation, the police had to let him go. No proof. No evidence.

Poor Dave, Melissa thought, remembering his troubled face, his nervous eyes, his trembling chin when he tried to explain it all to her.

Dave couldn't return to a normal life. No one would let him.

Too many people in Shadyside, too many of his own friends, believed that he was a murderer.

First, the cheating incident. Then Josie's murder. Then breaking into the McClains' house. Then the attack on Erica.

Even if the police couldn't prove it, most of the town believed Dave was guilty.

For his sake, Dave's parents moved and sent him away to a boarding school upstate. Dave was gone, but the rumors about him continued.

Melissa hated the way kids talked about Dave. How could they be so sure he was a murderer? Why were they so willing and eager to believe that Dave was guilty?

It all seemed so clear and simple to some kids Melissa knew. Dave had hated Josie. Everyone knew that.

When Josie turned him in for cheating and he got kicked off the wrestling team because of it, he went berserk and killed her. That was the story a lot of people believed.

Then he broke into the McClains' house to get his threatening valentines back. Erica caught him in the act. Dave didn't want her to tell the police about the valentines. So he tried to kill her too.

That was the story some people believed.

And Melissa?

Melissa didn't know what to believe. She knew Dave really well. She'd been dating him for a long time. He trusted her. He confided in her.

Dave had a wild, impulsive side, Melissa knew. And he had an angry side. Sending those threatening valentines was a really dumb, messed-up thing to do.

But Dave wasn't a murderer. Melissa *knew* him. He wasn't a murderer.

Was he?

Luke walked across the den and put his arms

around Melissa. He didn't say anything. His wool sweater felt scratchy against her cheek.

"Here it is a whole year later," Melissa said wistfully. "And there are still so many questions, so many unanswered questions."

"We have to try to put it behind us," Luke said softly.

"But how?" Melissa demanded.

He let go of her and shrugged. "I don't know." He lowered his eyes. "I still think about Rachel a lot," he confessed.

Outside the window the sky darkened as the heavy clouds continued to gather. The shadows on the den carpet lengthened as Melissa gazed at Luke. She suddenly felt as if the darkness was trying to swallow her up.

"I know it was hard for you," Melissa said softly. "To stop going over there, I mean."

He nodded solemnly. "It was harder on Rachel," he replied. "Erica told me it was a real setback for Rachel." His voice broke. "But what could I do? I had to get on with my life."

Luke stepped past Melissa and peered out the window, pressing both hands down on the window sill. The gray light glinted in his glasses. His eyes seemed wild, unfocused.

"I don't know *what* I was thinking," he said, talking to himself as much as to Melissa. "I mean, going over there every day. I guess I thought I was making a big difference in Rachel's life, helping her get better." He uttered a pained sigh. "It took me so long to realize that Rachel will *never* get better."

Melissa didn't reply for a long while. The den was blanketed in silence, silence and deepening shadows. A car door slammed somewhere down the block. Two dogs started to bark.

"I've become pretty friendly with Erica," Melissa said. "I go to visit Rachel every week, and then I stay and talk with Erica. I—I feel so sorry for her."

"What do you mean?" Luke asked softly, turning to face her.

"Well, it took her so long to recover from that knife wound. And—well—she seems so lonely. The McClains still can't afford a full-time nurse for Rachel, so—"

"Let's change the subject," Luke said sharply.

"Yeah, good idea," Melissa quickly agreed. "That was all a year ago. It's over. Done." She crossed the room to the desk and picked up the stack of mail.

"Do you know about the skating party?" Luke asked. "On Valentine's Day? At Fear Lake?"

"Ice-skating?" she asked, concentrating on the envelopes.

"No, roller-skating on ice," Luke joked, rolling his eyes.

"Huh? Sorry. I wasn't listening." Melissa lowered the envelopes and grinned at him. "What were you saying? Roller-skating on ice?"

Luke chuckled. "There's a Valentine's Day party on Fear Lake. A skating party. Do you want to go?"

"Yeah. Okay. Great," Melissa replied. Her grin faded. "Only, I'm a terrible skater. I spend more time on my butt than on my feet. Weak ankles, I guess."

"I'll give you some lessons," Luke promised. He

saw that she had turned her attention back to the mail. "Hey, what's that?"

"Looks like a card. For me," she replied, pleased. She started to pull the envelope open. "A valentine, I bet. Aren't you a little early, Luke?"

"I didn't send it," Luke protested, crossing the den with long strides, stepping up behind her to read it over her shoulder.

The front of the card was a bouquet of flowers. Melissa unfolded it and read the handwritten message. She gasped.

> Roses are red
> Violets are blue,
> On Valentine's Day
> You'll be dead too.

Chapter 21

MISSING

*E*rica stared into the dressing table mirror as she brushed Rachel's long, copper-colored hair. Outside Rachel's bedroom window, the gray clouds were lowering in the late-afternoon sky.

The radiator against the wall hissed noisily, the only sound other than the soft *whoosh* of the hairbrush through Rachel's long hair.

Erica, wearing faded jeans and an oversize gray sweatshirt, studied her sister's face in the mirror. She's so pretty, Erica thought. I wonder if she'll always be this pretty. I wonder if her face will stay as young as her mind.

Lowering her eyes, she noticed that Rachel was hugging something tightly in her hands. "What is that?" she asked her sister, breaking the tranquil silence. "What are you holding?"

Rachel held up the small brown teddy bear. Erica

recognized it at once. It was the teddy bear Luke had given Rachel more than a year ago.

Erica sighed, painful memories flooding back. Glancing at the small calendar on the wall beside Rachel's dressing table, Erica realized it was almost Valentine's Day.

She sighed again and started to brush harder, starting at the crown and pulling the brush down, down through the thick, straight red hair.

"It's just the two of us now, Rachel," Erica blurted out, thinking aloud.

"What?" Rachel asked, her voice surprisingly cold. "What did you say?" She sounded almost angry.

"Never mind," Erica muttered.

"Is Luke coming?" Rachel asked.

The question startled Erica momentarily. Rachel hadn't asked for Luke in weeks.

"Is Luke coming?" Rachel repeated impatiently.

"No," Erica told her softly. "Luke isn't coming anymore, remember? Luke is with Melissa now."

"I hate Melissa!" Rachel cried, violently pushing the hairbrush away. It flew out of Erica's hand and clattered across the floor.

"Rachel, calm down," Erica said, going to retrieve the brush.

"I *hate* Melissa! I *hate* Melissa! I *hate* Melissa!" Rachel chanted angrily, screaming more loudly each time.

"Rachel, please!" Erica pleaded. "Don't get worked up. I didn't mean for you to—"

"I *hate* Melissa! I *hate* Melissa!"

Erica cried out as she watched Rachel tear open the teddy bear in a rage. "I *hate* Melissa!" Rachel screamed, pulling handfuls of gray stuffing out of the opening she had ripped in the bear's stomach.

"Stop!" Erica lurched forward and grabbed the teddy bear out of Rachel's hand. There were clumps of stuffing in Rachel's lap. Rachel stopped chanting, but her features remained twisted in rage.

"Let's calm down, okay?" Erica pleaded, lowering her voice to a whisper. "Let me brush your hair, okay, Rachel? Nice and slow. The way you like it?"

"I hate Melissa, and I hate Luke," Rachel said a little calmer. She stared thoughtfully at her angry reflection in the mirror.

"No, Rachel. It isn't right to hate people," Erica said softly. "You've got to—"

The phone rang, interrupting her.

She started to the bedroom door. "I'll be right back. I'm just going to answer that," she told her sister.

Rachel didn't reply. She continued to study herself in the mirror, seeming to be fascinated by her own reflection.

Erica hurried down the hallway to the nearest phone, which was in her bedroom. Even though it was a year later, she was still surprised by the thick, new carpeting in the hall. The old carpet, stained with Erica's blood, had been replaced before she had returned from the hospital.

She felt a stab of pain in her side. It happened every time she walked down the hallway. A reminder. A painful reminder.

"Hello?" She picked up the phone, out of breath.

"Hi, Erica. It's me, Steve."

Erica gasped in surprise.

Steve Barron? Calling *her*?

Why on earth was Steve calling? Erica had barely spoken to him since Josie's death.

"Guess you're surprised to hear from me," Steve said, reading Erica's thoughts.

"Yeah. Uh—how *are* you?" she asked awkwardly.

"Okay. Good," he told her. "I've—well—I've been thinking about you. I saw you at school the other day. In the lunch room. And I—well . . ."

Why does he sound so nervous? Erica wondered, listening to him stammer. He always seemed to know the right thing to say around Josie.

"There's an ice-skating party on Fear Lake on the night of Valentine's Day," Steve said, speaking rapidly without taking a breath. "I thought maybe you might like to—uh—come with me."

Erica was stunned.

She felt her heart skip a beat.

How weird! she thought.

Steve Barron asking *me* out! He's a senior, and I'm only a sophomore. Besides, he never looked at me twice when Josie was alive.

"Yes, great," she replied breathlessly.

"Good," Steve said, sounding relieved. "The lake is almost completely frozen, so—"

"Oh, wait," Erica interrupted. She groaned unhappily. "I can't, Steve."

"Huh?"

"It's a Sunday, right? I can't go out that Sunday night. My mom has to go somewhere, and my dad will be away on a business trip. I promised I'd stay home to take care of Rachel."

There was a long silence at the other end.

"Oh, wow," Steve said finally. When he continued, he spoke with genuine concern. "You know, you have to have a life, too, Erica."

"Tell me about it," Erica said bitterly.

"No, really," Steve insisted. "You can't just spend your whole life . . ." His voice trailed off.

"I know, but what can I do?"

"It's going to be a nice party," Steve continued as if she hadn't said no. "Do you like to skate?"

"Yeah, I haven't done it for a while," Erica said wistfully.

"Well, maybe you could get someone else to stay with Rachel and—"

"I don't think so," Erica said, and then added, "Sorry."

She couldn't tell if Steve was hurt or angry. "Maybe some other time?" Erica asked hopefully.

"Yeah. Okay," Steve said brusquely. "Take care, okay?" He hung up before she could reply.

How strange, Erica thought, holding on to the receiver.

I never thought Steve even knew I was alive. I was just Josie's kid sister. The pest.

She replaced the receiver, feeling a wave of sadness wash over her. High school was supposed to be such an exciting time, she thought, uttering a loud sigh. But *I spend all my time in this creepy, old house, locked* up with Rachel. I've lost all my friends. I have no dates. I can't go out or do anything. I just stay here night after night, brushing Rachel's hair.

Remembering that she had left Rachel alone, Erica turned and stepped out into the hallway. She felt another stab of pain in her side, where the letter opener had injured her.

Ignoring it, she made her way to Rachel's room and hurried inside. "Rachel?"

No reply.

Erica stopped short when she saw that the chair in front of the dressing table was empty.

"Rachel?"

Silence.

Outside the window, the clouds had darkened to an eerie green-charcoal color. The bare trees shivered and shook.

Erica glanced quickly around the bedroom. "Rachel?"

No Rachel.

"Hey! Where'd you go?" The tremble in Erica's voice revealed her fear. "Rachel? Where'd you go? You weren't supposed to move!"

Feeling the beginnings of panic, Erica ran out of the room and down to the landing.

Wrapping one hand around the banister railing, she stared down the stairs to the front hall.

"Rachel?"

No reply.

Then to her horror Erica saw that the front door was wide open.

Chapter 22

DAVE IS GUILTY AGAIN

"Rachel? Rachel?"

Leaning against the banister, Erica bounded down the stairs, taking them two at a time.

What is Rachel's *problem?* she thought angrily as she pushed the storm door open with both hands and raced outside.

She *knows* she isn't allowed out without someone to watch her. Why is she so *odd* today?

"Rachel? Rachel?"

Swirling winds made the fat brown leaves dance across the front yard. The sky was nearly as dark as night.

"Rachel? Are you out here?"

Across the street, Erica could see Luke's car parked in Melissa's driveway. She felt the pain in her side again and shivered, chilled by the cold, swirling winds.

"Rachel? It's going to storm!"

Where is she? Am I going to have to call the police? No.

Rachel poked her head out from behind the gnarled trunk of a wide, old maple tree. "Hi, Erica." She stepped away from the tree, a pleased smile on her face.

"Rachel!" Erica shrieked angrily, her heart pounding in her chest. "What are you *doing* out here?"

Rachel came toward Erica, walking slowly, steadily, her long hair fluttering in the wind behind her like a copper-colored sail. "Did I scare you, Erica?" she asked, her grin widening.

"Huh?" Erica stared at her sister, startled.

"Did I scare you?" Rachel repeated, her green eyes sparkling with gleeful excitement. "Did I *really* scare you?"

Erica stared back at her sister, dread forming in the pit of her stomach. She shivered. From the cold? Or from the evil glee on Rachel's face?

"Did I scare you, Erica?"

What goes on in that mind of yours, Rachel, Erica wondered.

Erica put her arm around her sister's shoulders and gently guided her back into the house. As they entered the hallway, Rachel started to laugh. A dark, chilling laugh.

What do you know, Rachel? Erica wondered, staring intently at her sister. Do you know a lot more than you let on?

"Here, look at this," Melissa said. "Just read it." She pushed the card at Luke with a trembling hand.

It was Monday afternoon after school. Melissa had been home only long enough to open the new valentine and read it before Luke pulled into the drive.

Now, his coat still on, his red and white wool muffler still wrapped around his neck, he gazed at the card she had given him, waiting for his eyes to focus on the handwritten message.

> Flowers mean funerals
> Flowers mean death.
> On Valentine's Day
> You'll take your last breath.

He stared at the card, crinkling his eyes thoughtfully as if studying each word. Then he handed it back to Melissa, his expression one of concern. "You're upset?"

"I'm scared," she said flatly.

He started to unwrap the muffler. "It's probably a joke."

"It wasn't a joke for Josie," Melissa shot back.

He tossed the coat and muffler onto the banister and tugged at the bottom of his sweater. She led him into the kitchen. "Want some hot chocolate?" she asked, biting her lower lip. She reached for the tea kettle.

"Maybe you should call the police," he suggested, shoving his hands into the pockets of his black jeans.

"Maybe," Melissa replied, filling the kettle.

"Did you show the cards to your parents?" Luke asked, stepping up to the sink beside her.

Melissa nodded. "They think it's just a joke. A

really sick joke. Mom reminded me to keep the doors locked at all times, and to call the police at the slightest sound."

She put the kettle on the stove and turned on the burner. Then she turned to him, stood on tiptoes, and kissed him. "Happy Birthday," she said when the kiss had ended. She licked her lips.

"It isn't my birthday," Luke replied.

She chuckled. "So?"

He suddenly became very serious. He pulled off his glasses and rubbed the bridge of his nose. "Hey, I just got an idea."

The kettle started to rumble quietly.

"What kind of idea?" Melissa demanded.

"About the valentines," Luke said, carefully replacing his glasses. "Dave sent the ones last year, right? The ones to Josie."

"Yeah. Of course," Melissa replied impatiently.

"Well, do you think he's sending these cards to you?"

"Huh?" Melissa's mouth dropped open. She pulled at a strand of black hair. "Dave? Why?"

"I don't know why," Luke said patiently. "I just wonder if he's the one sending the cards. They sound just like the ones Josie got last year."

"Yeah, I guess," Melissa said. The kettle started to whistle. She grabbed the handle and lifted the kettle off the burner. "So what's your idea?" She pulled two white mugs down from the cabinet.

"You said you got a letter from Dave this week. Do you still have it?"

161

"Yeah, I guess," Melissa said, trying to remember where she put it. Her eyes lit up and she turned her gaze on him. "I get it! We compare the handwriting in Dave's letter to the handwriting on the valentines."

"Yeah, you've got it," Luke said.

"I think I left his letter on my desk," she said. She tossed two hot chocolate packets onto the counter. "Here, you make the drinks. I'll go get the letter and the cards."

She hurried out of the room.

It can't be Dave, she thought. No way.

Why would Dave send such hateful cards to me?

It can't be Dave.

She had begun scrambling through the papers on her desk, searching for Dave's letter, when the phone rang. Annoyed by the interruption, she picked up the receiver. "Hello?"

"Hello, Melissa?"

A woman's voice. Familiar, but Melissa didn't recognize it.

"Melissa, it's Marsha Kinley. Up in Portstown."

Dave's mom?

Why was Dave's mom calling Melissa? And why did she sound so upset?

"How are you, Mrs. Kinley?"

"Okay, Melissa. Have you seen Dave?" Mrs. Kinley asked, speaking breathlessly.

"Dave? Huh? No." Melissa's voice revealed her confusion. "Isn't Dave—?"

"He ran away," Mrs. Kinley interrupted. "From his boarding school. Last night. You haven't seen him?"

"No," Melissa told her. "Why would he come here?"

There was a short pause. The line crackled with static. "He's been talking about you lately, Melissa. A lot. I'm really worried. I don't know why he's run away. I hope he isn't going to get himself in more trouble."

Melissa suddenly realized she was gripping the receiver so hard that her hand ached. She forced herself to loosen her hold.

"And you really think he's coming to Shadyside?" she asked.

"I don't know," Mrs. Kinley replied, her voice tight with worry. "But please, call me if you see him, okay? Or if you hear from him. Or anything. Call me right away. Okay, Melissa?"

Melissa agreed and hung up.

She tugged at a strand of her hair, winding it and unwinding it around her finger. Mrs. Kinley's frightened voice remained in her ears.

"I hope he isn't going to get himself in more trouble," she had said, sounding so worried, so upset.

I hope so too, Melissa thought.

Remembering why she was up in her room, she began searching her desk again. She found Dave's letter in the top drawer and hurried downstairs with it.

"That was Dave's mom. On the phone," she told a startled Luke. "She said Dave ran away from school and he might be coming here. She didn't know. She sounded really freaked."

Luke shoved the hot chocolate mugs out of the way. Melissa plopped the two valentines down on the counter. Huddled together, the two of them studied the handwriting, moving from the cards to the letter, then back again.

"No doubt about it," Melissa said, gazing at Luke, her eyes widening in horror. "The handwriting is the same. Dave sent the valentines."

Luke stared down at the ugly messages on the cards. "It's the same handwriting okay," he muttered thoughtfully.

"And now Dave is coming here," Melissa said in a voice choked with horror. "He sent these cards to me. And now he's coming here. To make his threats come true."

Chapter 23

AN INTRUDER

Erica opened the front door and her eyes widened in surprise. "Melissa, hi!" she said, pushing open the glass storm door.

"How are you?" Melissa asked, wiping her shoes on the straw welcome mat before stepping into Erica's front hallway. The aroma of roasting chicken floated out from the kitchen, reminding Melissa that she was hungry.

"Okay," Erica replied, studying Melissa's face as if trying to determine the reason for her visit. "Did you come to see Rachel? I think she's taking a nap."

"No, I came to see you," Melissa said somberly, her voice nearly a whisper.

"Take off your coat," Erica said, reaching for it.

Melissa shook her head. "No, I can only stay a minute. It's almost dinner time." She glanced through the storm door behind her. Across the street, her dad's car was pulling up the drive. "My dad has to eat two minutes after he gets home," Melissa said, "or else he gets crabby."

Erica snickered. "So what's up?"

Melissa pushed her hair off her forehead. "I just wanted to tell you that Dave is missing from his school."

Even in the dim hall light, Melissa could see Erica turn pale. Erica gaped at Melissa for a long moment, as if trying to grasp what Melissa had just told her.

"He's missing?" she said finally. "You mean he ran away?"

"Yeah," Melissa replied, nodding. "His mom called me."

"You mean he's coming here?" Erica asked, her shock turning to fear.

"I don't know," Melissa said, shoving her hands into her coat pockets. "Maybe. I just thought I should tell you—"

"But he *can't!*" Erica declared shrilly, her face white, her eyes wide with fear. She had knotted her hands into tense fists at her side.

"I'm sorry," Melissa said, not sure why she was apologizing. She hadn't expected Erica to react with such fright.

"I've always thought Dave was the one," Erica said in a trembling voice. "The one who killed Josie. The one who attacked me last year." She glanced up the front stairway to the landing where she had been stabbed.

"But you told the police—" Melissa started.

"I couldn't tell them anything," Erica interrupted. "I didn't see who stabbed me. I didn't see anything.

But I always thought it was Dave. He had so much anger. So much hate. He sent my sister those awful valentines. Then he broke into our house . . ." Erica's voice trailed off. She swallowed hard.

Melissa glanced across the street. "I'd better be going. I just thought you should know that Dave—"

"Now he's coming back to finish the job," Erica muttered, consumed with fright. She shuddered violently. "He's coming back to do something terrible."

"I've been getting valentines too," Melissa told her. "Threatening valentines. Like Josie." She hadn't meant to reveal that to Erica. The words just came tumbling out.

"The same threats? You have?" Erica asked, gazing into Melissa's face with concern.

Melissa nodded. "Two of them so far," she said, whispering as Erica's mother crossed the hallway heading for the kitchen. "In Dave's handwriting."

Erica uttered a silent, frightened gasp. "Then is Dave coming here to kill *you?*" she asked.

"I want to go to sleep now," Rachel said, yawning.

Erica pulled the hairbrush one last time through her sister's long hair. Then she set the brush down on the dressing table.

She glanced at the clock on Rachel's bedside table. A little after eight-thirty. Time to start her homework. She had an oral report to give the next day and hadn't even started to rehearse it.

Rachel took up so much of her time these days, Erica thought with a bitter sigh.

She waited until Rachel had slipped under the

covers, said good night, and turned off the light. Then she headed downstairs to see if her mother needed anything before she started her homework.

Mrs. McClain was about to go out. "Your aunt Beth asked me to come over and look at some fabric samples," she explained, searching her bag for her car keys. "I won't be late."

"No problem," Erica replied. "Rachel's going to sleep."

Mrs. McClain pulled out the car keys. "Good news, Erica. Your father is coming home tomorrow. And I think he's going to *stay* home for a while."

"Great!" Erica said with enthusiasm. "I hardly remember what he looks like."

"Me either," her mother said, heading for the door. "I think he's tall. Or maybe he's short. I forget which."

They both laughed. Mrs. McClain blew her daughter a kiss, then disappeared out the door.

An hour later Erica was surrounded by books, sprawled on her stomach on the living room carpet, scribbling furiously on a long, legal-size pad, trying to get her report together.

Outside, the wind whistled and howled. The living room lights flickered for a moment, threatening to go out.

That's all I need, Erica thought. A power failure. I'd have to write my report by candlelight.

She gazed up at the ceiling fixture, expecting the light to go out. But the flickering stopped. The winds continued to howl, a shrill, lonely sound like an animal call.

A few minutes later Erica heard other sounds. She raised her head, dropping her pen to the rug.

The sounds were coming from the den.

Somebody had bumped into something.

Somebody was in there.

Erica raised herself to her knees. And listened.

Another footstep. A creaking floorboard.

"Who's there?" she called.

Silence.

"Rachel, is that you? Did you wake up?"

No reply.

"Rachel? Answer me."

It isn't Rachel, she realized. But it's someone. Someone in the den.

And I'm all alone here.

Gripped with fear, she struggled to her feet. Her heart pounding against her chest. Outside, the wind howled even louder, as if crying out a warning.

"Who—who's there?" Erica stammered.

Silently tip-toeing, she made her way to the den door. She stopped just outside the doorway and listened. Then, timidly, she poked her head into the room—and cried out.

Chapter 24

ANOTHER INTRUDER

Erica bolted into the den, sputtering angrily. "Luke, what are *you* doing here?" she demanded.

Startled, Luke took a step back from the desk, his face bright red. "Hi, Erica. I—uh . . ."

"What are you doing here?" Erica repeated, stopping a few feet in front of him, glaring at him, her fists angrily pushed against her hips.

"Sorry," Luke muttered uncomfortably. "I was just—leaving a valentine for Rachel." He held up the square white envelope he had in his right hand.

"Huh? A valentine?" Erica lowered her eyes to the card. "But why did you sneak in?"

"I—I didn't want to disturb anyone," Luke explained, his face still scarlet, his expression guilty, embarrassed. "I mean, I saw you studying so hard and I guessed Rachel was asleep. So I was just going to leave this and scoot."

Erica studied his face, trying to determine if he was telling the truth. "You scared me to death," she said, exhaling loudly. "If I was a cat, that would've been all nine lives."

"Sorry," Luke repeated softly. "I didn't mean to. Really."

"You feel guilty, don't you," Erica accused, crossing her arms in front of her chest, locking her eyes on his.

"Huh? Guilty?"

"Yeah." She refused to soften her gaze, even though he looked away. "Guilty. Guilty about Rachel."

"Give me a break, Erica," Luke said, pleading.

"Do you know what happened to Rachel after you stopped coming? Do you have any idea how devastated she was?" Erica cried.

"I—I can't talk about it," Luke stammered. "I still care about Rachel, but I'm with Melissa now. Here."

He tossed the valentine at Erica and ran past her out of the den, into the hall and out of the house without looking back once.

Across the street Melissa was playing perhaps the most boring game of Scrabble in the history of the universe. "Daddy, can't we quit?" she begged. "You're ahead by four hundred points because I've had nothing but vowels the whole night!"

Mr. Davis chuckled, leaning over the table, his eyes lowered to his line of letters. "That's not why you're losing, Beanpole. You're losing because I'm a good

171

defensive player. You have to have a strong defense in Scrabble. Most people don't know that."

"Don't call me Beanpole," Melissa grumbled. "You know I hate it." She shoved her letters around on the holder, frowning. "Want me to call you Fatso?"

Mr. Davis raised his head abruptly. "Don't you dare." He was a big bear of a man, weighing around two hundred pounds, and was very sensitive about his weight.

"I can't make a word," Melissa wailed. "All I have are *O*'s and *U*'s."

Mr. Davis glanced at the score sheet. "Okay, Melissa. We can quit. You always were a poor loser," he teased.

Melissa uttered a cry of frustration and shoved the board across the table causing the pieces to tumble out of place.

"Loser cleans up," her father declared, grinning. "I'm going to watch the news. It's nearly eleven." He pushed himself away from the kitchen table and, after stopping at the refrigerator for a snack, headed into the den to join Melissa's mom.

Grumbling to herself, Melissa cleaned up the game, then headed up to her room.

Two hours later she was still struggling to fall asleep. Forcing her eyes to remain closed, she tried to think pleasant, soothing thoughts. She pictured Luke. His shy smile. The way his light brown hair curled just above his ears. How cute he looked in his silver-framed glasses.

She tried counting sheep. Fluffy white, four-legged

cottonballs. She pictured them hopping over a low fence, just like in the cartoons.

Whoever thought up counting sheep as a way to get to sleep? she wondered. What a dumb idea. Did it ever work?

She tried counting puppy dogs. Then she tried to clear all the animals out of her mind and concentrate on nothing at all. Sheer nothingness.

Clear, white nothingness. Soft nothingness.

She had just about drifted off to sleep when she heard a loud *thump* outside her window.

"Huh?"

She sat up, instantly alert.

"Hey!"

Am I asleep? Am I dreaming? Melissa asked herself uncertainly.

No.

Someone was there, outside her window. Balanced on a tree limb.

Gaping in fright, Melissa could see someone out there, blocking the light from the street lamp, arms at the sides of her window.

"Who's there? What's happening?"

She tried to move, tried to scramble out of bed.

But fear had paralyzed her. She could only raise her hands to her face.

Then her window was pulled open.

A dark figure dropped into her room with a groan, landing heavily on the carpet.

"Oh!"

Melissa opened her mouth to scream, but no sound came out.

He advanced toward her, arms stiff at his sides, a shadow moving in shadows.

As he came near, his face loomed out of the darkness. His eyes were cold, his features set.

"Dave!" Melissa cried in a tight, frightened voice. "Dave, stop! What are you doing?"

Chapter 25

THE REAL KILLER

*B*reathing hard, Dave stopped beside Melissa's bed. His dark eyes glared down at her. In the dim light from the window, she saw that he was even thinner, his scraggly hair falling past his shoulders now.

"Melissa," he whispered, still trying to catch his breath. "You look so scared."

"You—yes—" she stammered, finally finding her voice. She gripped the covers and pulled them up to her shoulders.

"So you think I'm guilty too," he said, his voice filled with menace and disappointment.

"No, Dave—"

"That's why you're scared, huh?" he asked, leaning over her, so close she could smell onions on his breath. "You're scared of me because you think I killed Josie?"

"No," Melissa replied angrily. "I'm scared because you broke into my house. I'm scared because you climbed in my window like—like a burglar or something!"

He snickered. "Sorry."

Melissa climbed out of bed and crossed the room to her closet, keeping her eyes on Dave. Feeling around in the dark closet, she found her robe, and pulled it on, struggling with one sleeve.

"Why'd you climb in here like that, Dave? What are you doing?" she demanded, clicking on the ceiling light.

They both blinked under the sudden brightness.

Dave looked terrible, she saw. His eyes were red rimmed, with dark circles under them. His hair was greasy and disheveled, his sweater and jeans wrinkled and filthy.

"I always wondered if you believed me," he said, ignoring her questions. "I always wondered if you thought I killed Josie. If you thought I stabbed Erica. You said you believed me. But I always wondered."

"I *did* believe you!" Melissa insisted, keeping her back against the wall, edging nervously toward the doorway. "You *know* I believed you."

"I don't know *what* I know," he said bitterly.

"Dave, what are you doing here now? What do you want?"

"I just happened to be in the neighborhood," he replied, snickering at his own joke. He dropped down wearily on the edge of her bed and wiped his forehead with the dirty sleeve of his sweater. "That tree isn't easy to climb," he muttered.

"Dave, why did you run away from school? Your mother called me. She—"

"She did?" He slapped his forehead. "She spoiled my surprise?"

Melissa groaned impatiently. "Dave, she sounded very worried about you. Very frightened."

"You know Mom," he replied dryly, rolling his eyes.

"Dave, why?" Melissa insisted. "Why'd you come back?"

"Okay, okay. I'll tell you why I'm here," he said, suddenly turning serious. "I didn't come here to scare you, Melissa. I've missed you, you know."

"I-I've missed you too," Melissa said awkwardly, leaning back against the wall, relaxing a little and sighing.

"I heard about you and Luke," Dave said flatly, without any expression at all.

"Well . . ."

"I was kind of surprised," he said, his cheeks flushing pink.

"Me too," Melissa confessed. "But you didn't come here because of Luke, did you?"

"I think I know who the real killer is," he said abruptly, staring up at her, his dark eyes flashing to life. "I've had so much time to figure it out, so much time to think about it. I can't get it out of my mind. I'm obsessed with clearing my name, with finding the real killer."

"That's why you've come back to Shadyside?" Melissa asked.

He nodded. "I want to prove that I'm not a killer. I want to prove it to you. To everybody."

"Then why did you send me those disgusting valentines?" Melissa snapped, the words bursting angrily from her.

"Huh?" He jumped to his feet in surprise. "What valentines? What are you talking about?"

"Don't act innocent," Melissa said sharply. "You know what valentines. The ones with the ugly threats. Just like you sent to Josie."

"Huh?" He scratched his greasy hair, his eyes studying her face. "Melissa, you don't think that I—"

"Come off it, Dave," Melissa shouted. "You sent them to me. They're in your handwriting."

"Get real," he muttered, shaking his head. "You're messed up. Really."

She glared at him angrily but didn't reply, waiting for him to drop the innocent act and confess.

"Show them to me," he demanded. "Get them. I want to see."

"Fine. Here." She pulled open the top drawer of her desk, grabbed the two valentines, and tossed them at him.

They fell to the floor beside his muddy sneakers. He bent to pick them up. Then holding them close to his face, he examined them carefully, reading each one again and again, squinting as he studied the handwriting.

When he finally finished and set the cards down on the bed, Melissa saw that he was breathing heavily, his eyes glowing with excitement. "Now I *know* who the killer is!" he exclaimed, leaping to his feet.

"Who?" Melissa demanded.

He didn't seem to hear her. Lost in his own thoughts, he hurried to the open window, and pulled his knees onto the windowsill as he reached for the tree branch.

"Who?" Melissa repeated. "Who is it, Dave? Tell me!"

Without replying, without a goodbye, he dropped out of view, scrambling down the tree trunk.

"Who is it? Who?" she called after him, leaning out into the cold, still night.

But he had disappeared into the darkness.

Chapter 26

LONG RED HAIR

"Where is Erica?" Rachel asked.

Melissa took Rachel's hand and led her down the driveway. "Erica is at school," she replied. "She had to stay late today. She's rehearsing a play. She asked me to take care of you."

"I go to school too," Rachel said, smiling.

"It's such a pretty day," Melissa said, holding Rachel's hand as they walked. "I thought it might be nice to take a walk."

"I'm very smart in my school," Rachel said proudly.

The late-afternoon sun, still high over the winter-bare trees, felt surprisingly warm. The soft breeze more like spring than early February.

Abruptly Rachel pulled her hand out of Melissa's. "I can go outside by myself," she said crossly.

Melissa smiled at her, concealing her surprise at

Rachel's sudden anger. "Really? Do you go out by yourself a lot?"

Rachel didn't reply for a long while. They descended the driveway and turned right, walking up Fear Street, which was silent and deserted except for the excited cries of a group of children playing some kind of game in a backyard down the block.

"I *can,*" Rachel insisted suddenly. "I *can* go outside by myself."

"That's nice," Melissa told her as a wave of sadness swept over her. Poor Rachel, she thought. She used to be so terrific, really popular, smart, a great student, a great friend.

She was still beautiful, though, as beautiful as any fashion model. But there was something missing behind her eyes. She became more and more like a dreamy child.

"Oh, look!" Rachel cried suddenly.

"Wait!" Melissa called.

Rachel ignored her and ran full speed toward a big mound of dead brown leaves near the curb. Laughing gleefully, Rachel dove into the pile, thrashing her arms wildly as if swimming in them.

Melissa had to laugh, watching Rachel's innocent joy.

Flopping around in the leaf pile, Rachel was having the time of her life.

It was so sad, so tragic, and so touching all at the same time.

"Hey Rachel—make room!" Melissa cried. She took a running dive into the pile too. Rachel laughed gleefully. The two of them had a rousing leaf fight, rolling around, tossing handfuls of leaves, laughing together.

About half an hour later Melissa and Rachel were in the front yard playing catch with a large rubber ball when Erica arrived. "Hey, what's going on?" she asked Melissa, surprised to find them outdoors.

"It was such a pretty day," Melissa said, smiling. "Rachel and I have been having fun."

"You have to watch her really carefully outdoors," Erica said nervously.

"I can go outside by myself!" Rachel insisted.

"No, you can't," Erica scolded. "You have to wait for someone to *take* you outside. Remember?"

Rachel frowned and didn't reply. She dropped the ball to the ground and kicked it toward the house.

"It was nice of you to watch her so I could go to rehearsal," Erica told Melissa. "I hope she wasn't too much trouble."

"No trouble at all," Melissa replied. Then she added, "I saw Dave last night."

Erica paled at the sound of his name. She raised her eyes to Melissa's, her expression troubled. "What did he say? What did he want?"

"He says he knows who killed Josie," Melissa told her. "He's come back to clear his name."

"Who?" Erica demanded eagerly. "Who killed Josie? Who? Who stabbed me?"

Melissa frowned. "He wouldn't say. He just said he knew."

Rachel laughed suddenly, a loud, mocking laugh. "Someone hates Erica," she sang. Then she began to chant it over and over. "Someone hates Erica. Someone hates Erica. . . ."

"Come on," Erica said, putting an arm gently around Rachel's slender shoulders. "Let's get you inside. Say goodbye to Melissa."

Melissa called goodbye, then turned and jogged across the street to her house. The sun was a glowing red ball now, lowering itself behind the trees. The air had taken on an evening chill.

"Hey!" She was startled to find Luke coming around the side of the house.

"Hi," he said somewhat shyly.

"Hi," she repeated, staring at him curiously. "What a nice surprise."

"Well, yeah. It's a surprise for me too," he said, an odd grin spreading across his face. His glasses glinted, catching the red glow of the sun. "Guess what I did?"

She stopped and stared at him. "You won the lottery?"

He laughed dryly. "Guess again."

"I can't guess. Why do you look so sheepish?"

"I locked myself out," he explained with a shrug. "I must have left my keys in school or something." He rolled his eyes. "Dumb or what? I couldn't get into my house, so I came over here."

"Well, I'm glad you're dumb!" she replied, grinning. "I've been taking care of Rachel. Now I guess I'll have to take care of you!"

She reached into her coat pocket for her keys. Not finding them, she reached into her other pocket. Then, a disconcerted look formed on her face as she searched her jeans pockets.

"Guess what?" she wailed, holding up her empty hands. "No keys. I'm dumb too!"

"We're both dumb," Luke agreed, smiling.

"Come here, Dummy." Melissa put her arms around his neck and gave him a long, enthusiastic kiss. "We make a good team," she said, leaning against his chest.

She kissed him again, wrapping her arms around his waist.

When the kiss ended, she raised her eyes to his. "You know, I really do think we make a good team," she said seriously.

Melissa felt very happy. But to her surprise, Luke seemed very embarrassed and more than a little troubled.

A little after eleven that night, Melissa was studying up in her room. Hunched over her desk, the small desk lamp casting a circle of light onto her open textbook, she struggled to concentrate.

She yawned and rubbed her tired eyes. She stretched her arms high over her head.

Then she heard sounds down in the front yard.

A *thud*. Followed by rapid footsteps. Followed by the *clang* of a metal garbage can toppling over onto the drive.

Startled, Melissa leapt to her feet, knocking over the desk chair as she scrambled to the window.

Is it Dave again?

That was her first thought.

Is he climbing up to my room again?

Has he fallen out of the tree?

It was such a warm night, she had left her bedroom window open.

Tingling with fear, Melissa peered out. The roof over the porch blocked her view of the driveway, but she could see a figure running away from the house. Running toward the street.

"Who is *that?*" Melissa cried out loud, squinting into the darkness.

Melissa couldn't see the face of the girl running across her front yard. All she could see was the long red hair trailing behind her.

Chapter 27

"NOT LUKE!"

"*I* don't believe it!" Melissa muttered, squinting against the darkness.

She heard a car roar away, its tires squealing.

I saw Rachel, she told herself, the night air cold against her hot cheeks. I saw Rachel running across the yard.

But that's impossible.

And whose car sped away? Did Rachel get into it? Rachel can't drive.

And why would Rachel drive anyway? She lives right across the street.

Feeling confused and upset, Melissa moved away from the window. Her heart was pounding. She suddenly felt chilled all over.

Rachel? Running outdoors? By herself in the middle of the night?

As she pulled on her robe, Melissa realized that her

parents were awake. "Melissa!" Her father's heavy footsteps thundered in the hallway. "Melissa, are you all right?"

He poked his head into her room, the door swinging open, the yellow hall light revealing him in pajama bottoms, his hair disheveled, his expression worried. "Are you okay?" he asked, surprised to find her standing by her closet. "I heard a prowler. I called the police."

"I—I heard it too," Melissa told him. She started to tell him that she saw Rachel running across the yard. But he was already halfway down the stairs.

Melissa tied her robe and headed to the stairway, nearly colliding with her mother on the stairs. "Your father called the police," she told Melissa, flashing a tense frown at her daughter.

They hurried down the stairs. The living room lights had been turned on. The hall and kitchen were also lit up. Mr. Davis had turned on all the lights in the house.

"The doors are locked," he called to them, sounding bewildered. "No sign of a break-in."

"Then what on earth—" Mrs. Davis started, following his voice to the kitchen.

Melissa's father was peering out the kitchen window at the garage. "Everything looks normal out there," he reported. "Garage door is closed."

Shivering, Mrs. Davis wrapped her arms around herself. "Weird," she muttered.

"I saw Rachel McClain outside," Melissa finally managed to say.

Both her parents turned to stare at her, squinting in disbelief. "What did you just say?" Mr. Davis asked, scratching his head.

"I saw her. I saw Rachel. She was running across the yard," Melissa insisted.

"But that's impossible," her mother said quickly, still hugging herself.

Mr. Davis stepped behind his wife and put an arm around her shoulders. "You must have been dreaming," he told Melissa, staring hard at her.

"But I *saw* her!" Melissa said shrilly. "I heard a noise. A crash. I ran to the window, and—"

"But Rachel isn't allowed out by herself," Mrs. Davis said. "She *can't* go out by herself."

"What would Rachel be doing in our yard?" Mr. Davis added. He shook his head. "Come on, Melissa—"

Melissa angrily pounded her fist on the kitchen counter. "I'm *not* crazy!" she shouted. "I saw Rachel out there!"

They didn't have any time to discuss it further. A loud knocking on the front door startled them all.

Melissa got to the front door first. "Who is it?" she called timidly.

"Police," replied a deep voice on the other side of the door.

Melissa pulled the door open to reveal two solemn-faced police officers. She stared at them in the harsh porch light. One was heavy, bald, and paunchy with an enormous, lumpy nose that resembled a potato. His partner was young and blond.

Melissa pushed open the storm door. The two officers stepped past her into the hallway.

"I called you because—" Mr. Davis started, stepping between Melissa and her mother.

"When did you discover the body?" the older policeman interrupted.

"What?" Mr. Davis asked, terribly confused.

"When did you discover the body?" the policeman repeated patiently, in a low, steady voice.

"What body?" Mrs. Davis asked, as bewildered as her husband.

"The body of the teenage boy on your driveway," the officer replied.

"No!" The scream burst from Melissa, more a shriek of horror than a word. *"No! Not Luke! Please, don't let it be Luke!"*

Chapter 28

STABBED

Erica yawned loudly as she pulled back the bedcovers. She glanced at the clock beside her bed.

I'm so tired. It's so late, she thought. I'll never be able to get up in time for school tomorrow.

Straightening the hem of her nightshirt, she eased herself into bed. The sheets felt cool. She knew she'd be able to fall asleep quickly.

She had nearly drifted off when the crackling of the intercom on the wall startled her awake. She sat up, immediately alert.

"Erica? Erica?" Rachel's voice broke through the late-night silence.

Rachel sounds wide awake, Erica thought.

What is she doing up at this hour?

"Erica, please come brush my hair."

Doesn't she have any idea how late it is? Erica wondered, rolling her eyes in exasperation.

No, of course she doesn't.

But why is she awake?

"Erica, please come brush my hair," Rachel repeated.

Erica groaned and climbed to her feet. "I'm coming, Rachel," she called into the intercom.

Yawning, she wearily made her way down the narrow hall to Rachel's room. Rachel was sitting up in bed, the bedside lamp on. She smiled as Erica entered. The soft light made Rachel's hair gleam.

"Brush out my hair?" Rachel asked.

"Rachel, it's so late," Erica moaned, yawning into her hand.

"I'm not sleepy," Rachel replied.

"But *I* am," Erica protested.

"Brush my hair. Just for a short while."

Erica moaned again, but picked up the hairbrush and climbed onto the bed on her knees beside Rachel. "Why aren't you sleepy?" she asked as she started to brush with long, slow strokes.

"I'm just not," Rachel replied brightly. "I'm wide awake."

"You may be wide awake now, but you're going to be exhausted tomorrow," Erica said wearily. She was so tired, it took a supreme effort to raise the hairbrush to Rachel's hair.

The front doorbell rang.

"Huh?" Erica cried out in surprise, dropping the brush.

"More," Rachel urged. "Brush some more."

"I can't. I'll be right back," Erica said, climbing off the bed. "There's someone at the door."

"Hurry back," Rachel instructed.

Erica's mother, wrapping a heavy wool sweater around her nightgown, was already at the front door when Erica got downstairs. "Who can it be at this hour?" she asked, hesitating with her hand on the doorknob.

Erica shrugged. "Rachel is awake," she told her mother. "Strange night, huh?"

"Oh," Mrs. McClain uttered a soft cry of surprise as she pulled the door open and saw the two police officers.

"Mrs. McClain?" the older, heavyset one asked, narrowing his eyes to peer into the entryway.

"Yes?" Mrs. McClain replied, her expression changing from surprise to fear. She pulled the sweater tighter around her shoulders.

"We need to speak to your daughter," he said.

"She's right here," Mrs. McClain said, flashing Erica a bewildered glance. She opened the glass storm door to allow the men to enter.

They ducked their heads as they came into the entryway even though the ceiling was high. "Are you Rachel McClain?" the older officer asked Erica.

"Huh? No," Erica replied, surprised. "Rachel is my sister." She motioned up the stairs.

"We need to talk to your sister Rachel," the officer said softly, raising his eyes to the stairway.

"But why?" Mrs. McClain demanded, pushing back a strand of hair that had fallen over her forehead.

"Well . . ." The officer hesitated and glanced at his partner. The younger man cleared his throat but didn't say anything. "Well," the older one started again, "we need to talk to Rachel in connection with the death this evening of a young man named"—he checked his notepad—"Dave Kinley."

"Dave?" Erica cried. "Dead? How? I don't *believe* it!" She covered her face with her hands and slumped down to sit on the bottom step.

"Are you okay, miss?" the younger officer asked, bending over her.

"Dave?" Erica cried. "Dave is *dead?*"

"I'm sorry," the older man said softly. "I didn't mean to shock you. I didn't know how else to tell you."

"How awful," Mrs. McClain said, shaking her head, her voice a hushed whisper. "How awful."

Slumped on the bottom stair, Erica's hands remained over her face. "How?" she asked weakly. "What happened?"

"We found him across the street," the policeman offered. "In the Davises' driveway. Beside the front porch." He glanced at his pad. "The victim was stabbed to death. Very recently, we think. Our investigators are on their way."

"Stabbed?" Erica let out a terrified cry. She lowered her hands. Her face was bright red. "Stabbed? Just like my sister Josie? Just like me?"

Her mother leaned over and placed both hands comfortingly on her shoulders.

"May we talk to your daughter Rachel?" the younger officer, shifting his weight uncomfortably, asked Mrs. McClain.

"Rachel? Why Rachel?" Mrs. McClain demanded,

holding on to Erica, who was trembling and shaking her head.

"Someone fitting her description was observed fleeing the Davises' yard."

"That's impossible!" Erica cried.

Mrs. McClain's expression hardened. She clenched her jaw. "You've made a mistake," she said firmly. "My daughter could not have been the one."

"We need to talk to her for just a minute," the officer said, returning Mrs. McClain's stare.

"My daughter was in an accident," Mrs. McClain told them, her voice quivering. "Her brain was—damaged. She cannot leave the house by herself. She must always be watched."

"I'm sorry to insist," the older officer said softly. "But we have to talk to Rachel. We'll keep it very brief. Could you wake her for us?"

"She's awake," Erica said, climbing to her feet.

"You're wasting your time," Mrs. McClain insisted. "Rachel was not out of this house. Rachel couldn't stab anyone."

"I'm sure it's a misunderstanding," the man said.

Erica started up the stairs, followed by her mother, followed by the two officers. The stairs creaked noisily under all the weight.

Rachel was still sitting up in her bed, the covers up to her waist, her red hair falling softly against the headboard. "Hi," she said brightly as the officers stepped into the room.

"This is my daughter Rachel," Mrs. McClain told them, hurrying to Rachel's side and putting a hand on her slender shoulder.

"My sister has to be watched," Erica said, walking to the opposite side of the bed. "She cannot go out by herself."

"Yes, I *can!*" Rachel protested, smiling at the two police. "I go out all the time!"

Chapter 29

ANOTHER BROKEN HEART

"*E*rica, hi. How are you feeling?"

Erica made her way around a group of laughing kids and walked over to Melissa's locker. It was a few days later, Friday after school, and the hall was clearing out quickly.

"I'm better," Erica said, adjusting her backpack. "I—I had a couple of bad days," she admitted, lowering her eyes to the floor. "The doctor made me stay home. It was all such a shock. The news about Dave. The police suspecting Rachel. It was all so upsetting."

"Have the police come up with a lead?" Melissa asked, leaning back against a locker. "Anything at all?"

"I don't think so," Erica told her, sighing. "Of course, after they talked to Rachel for a few minutes, they realized that she couldn't have killed Dave. They realized immediately . . ." Her voice trailed off sadly. She chewed hard on her bubble gum.

"I can't believe they haven't turned up anything," Melissa said, tugging nervously at a strand of her hair. "It—it's so horrible. Right in my driveway. I—I just don't know what to think." She took a deep breath and lowered her hand. "Where you headed?"

"*Guys and Dolls* rehearsal," Erica replied. "I tried out for Adelaide, but I didn't get it." She sighed. "But at least I'm in the chorus. Are you going to the skating party on the lake Sunday night?"

"Yeah." Melissa nodded. "I don't really feel in a partying mood. But Luke is insisting we go. He says otherwise we'll just sit around and be morbid."

"*Morbid.*" Erica repeated the word, frowning. "Yeah. Morbid. I'm going too."

"Oh, yeah?" Melissa replied, pushing herself away from the locker, standing up straight. "Who's your date?"

Erica made a face. "I don't have one. I just thought I'd go to get out of the house. It's pretty *morbid* at my house too, you know." A dry, mirthless laugh escaped her lips. "Got to run. I'm already late."

Melissa watched Erica hurry down the long corridor.

Poor kid. She doesn't have it easy, Melissa thought.

Josie's face flashed into her mind. It would be so *horrible* to lose a sister, Melissa thought with a shudder.

So horrible to have a sister murdered.

One sister murdered. One sister stabbed. One sister's life ruined forever by a stupid accident.

The McClains don't have it easy, Melissa realized. Poor Erica.

She turned to her locker and began to spin the lock. Finishing the combination, she lifted up on the handle and pulled the door open.

And uttered a startled cry.

"Oh no!"

On the inside of the locker door, someone had painted a large, broken valentine heart. Smeared dots of bright red blood dripped from the heart. Scrawled in thick red paint at the bottom were the words: **YOU'RE DEAD.**

Chapter 30

THE PARTY

"*T*his is so romantic," Melissa said, grabbing Luke's arm and leaning close to him as they walked through the darkness.

Luke had parked on Fear Street, and now they were making their way along the winding path through the woods toward the lake, their ice skates draped over their shoulders.

Torches had been set up all along the lakefront. As they approached the lake, they saw the orange torch-light flickering in the spaces between the dark trees, giving the woods a soft, magical glow.

"Such a clear night. It's perfect!" Melissa declared.

"It's kind of pretty," Luke admitted as the frozen lake came into view.

"You're so poetic," Melissa teased, squeezing his arm through his jacket.

They could hear the music now, from a portable

sound system on the shore. And they could see several couples skating in a wide circle over the ice.

"How many of you *are* there in that coat?" Luke asked, laughing. He pulled at the side of Melissa's wool overcoat, stretching it wide.

Melissa laughed. "You don't like my coat? It's my dad's, actually." She lowered her head to examine it. "Maybe it *is* a little big. But I figured I might need the extra padding."

"Maybe later I'll climb in there with you!" Luke teased, letting go of the enormous coat and leading the way along the path to the lake.

Voices called to them as they drew nearer. People were clustered at a long refreshment table. Others were seated on the ground, struggling to fasten their skates. The woods echoed with laughter and voices shouting over the blare of the music.

"I warned you. I'm not a great skater," Melissa said, as Luke helped her tighten her laces. She glanced up at the skaters circling the lake, recognizing most of them. They all seemed so graceful, so at ease.

"Look at Cory Brooks," Luke said, pointing. She followed Luke's gaze across the ice to see Cory showing off as usual, skating backward on one leg, in the opposite direction from everyone else, his hands high above his head.

"What a showoff," Luke muttered. Then he burst out laughing as Cory collided with David Metcalf, and the two of them toppled to the ice, nearly sliding all the way to the refreshment table on their backsides.

Luke stopped laughing when he caught the serious

expression on Melissa's face. "Hey, what's wrong? You can't possibly be as bad a skater as Cory!"

"I—I wasn't thinking about that," Melissa said solemnly. She reached up for Luke to pull her to her feet. "I was thinking about my locker. That disgusting broken heart. The threatening valentines."

"Hey, I thought we were going to party tonight," Luke scolded.

Melissa sighed. "I know. But maybe it was a mistake. Maybe we shouldn't have come."

Gripping both of her gloved hands, he tugged her onto the lake. "I'm right here," he said softly, reassuring her with a smile. "Come on. Forget that nonsense. It's so awesome here tonight." He gestured to the flickering torches casting their soft light along the shore. "Let's just skate and have a good time."

"Okay," Melissa agreed, smiling back at him.

They skated side by side for a short while, picking their way through the crowd of skaters. Melissa moved unsteadily, her arms out awkwardly at her sides.

Like a toddler just starting to walk, she thought, embarrassed.

Luke moved across the ice with confident, graceful strides.

He looks so much more at ease on ice than when he's walking, Melissa thought, studying him as she tried to keep up.

"Stay away from over there!" someone called to them, pointing to the empty area to the right.

"What's the problem?" Luke called.

"The ice is too thin. It's already cracking!" came the reply.

Luke turned, making a wide circle. He reached for Melissa, but her left skate hit something, and she tumbled forward.

"Ow!"

She stretched out her hands to break her fall and landed hard on her right elbow. Pain shot up her arm. "Ow. Oh, man!"

"You okay?" Luke circled her, backing around her, reaching down to pull her back on her feet.

"I warned you," she said, frowning. Her side still throbbed, but she allowed him to pull her up. "Not exactly graceful, am I? My skate caught on something."

"You're a graceful faller," he said, teasing. "You stumble like a pro. Really."

"Liar," she muttered.

They started again, gliding side by side to the music. They skated in a wide oval over the frozen lake, their breath steaming up above them, the torches on shore providing the only light, casting long, shifting shadows over the ice.

"Hey, wait up!" Melissa called.

Luke, skating easily, had picked up speed and had moved far ahead. Concentrating on keeping her balance, Melissa kept losing him in the crowd.

"Wait up!" Then she fell again. Her skates slid right out from under her, and she landed hard on her back.

"Hey, Luke."

He appeared from out of the shadows and glided

202

easily up to her. "How'd you get down there?" he teased, bending to help her up once again.

"I'm going to be black and blue," she said. "It's my ankles, I think. They're not strong enough."

"Follow me," Luke said, skating away from the crowd.

She started to follow, moving slowly, one skate then the other, having lost all confidence. "Hey, where are you going?" she called.

"I'm going to give you a lesson," he called back.

He was leading her away from the crowd, away from the flickering torchlight, away from the music.

"Why are we going over here for the lesson?" she called, picking up speed.

"It's a *private* lesson!" he declared.

He skated into the darkness. She followed the *skud skud skud* of his skates.

It was so dark away from the lights. Away from the party.

Away from everyone.

She heard a cracking sound to her left.

"Hey, Luke!" she called, fear beginning to rise in her chest. "Luke, the ice! It's cracking!"

Then she remembered the warning to stay away from this area.

"Luke, we shouldn't be here!" she called, feeling her throat tighten and her heart begin to pound.

So dark. So silent.

Another *crack* just behind her.

Luke abruptly appeared out of the darkness, skating toward her, his features set, his eyes locked menacingly on hers.

Why has he led me here? Melissa wondered, suddenly consumed with fear.

Why did he take me to this dangerous spot, away from everyone else?

She spun around. Nearly fell. Started to skate back toward the party.

But he swept up behind her and grabbed her shoulders.

He twirled her around to face him.

Behind his glasses, his eyes gleamed with excitement.

"Luke, what are you *doing?*" Melissa cried.

Chapter 31

A HOODED FIGURE

Luke slid his hands down from Melissa's shoulders and wrapped them around her waist. Then he lowered his head and kissed her.

"I just wanted to get you alone," he whispered, starting to kiss her again.

"Get off me!" Melissa shouted angrily. She shoved him with both hands.

He slid backward, easily regaining his balance. His smile faded. "Melissa, what's your problem?"

"You scared me to *death!*" she cried angrily. "How could you be so insensitive?"

"I thought this was supposed to be a party," Luke snapped back, pouting. "I just—"

"You just forgot that I got all those death threats!" Melissa snapped.

"I thought—"

"You thought it was funny to lead me out here to the

darkest spot where the ice is cracking! I don't *believe* you!" She uttered an angry cry, raising her fists and nearly toppling over.

"Okay, okay. I was wrong," Luke said, raising both gloved hands as if to shield himself. "Cool off, okay? Just chill."

Melissa cast him a dirty look, but her anger had started to fade.

Luke was just trying to be romantic, after all.

But he scared her. He really scared her.

And besides, they had no business being out where the ice was thin and cracking.

"Why don't you skate on without me?" she suggested, softening her tone but unwilling to let him off the hook entirely. "Go ahead. Skate a few laps. I'm just slowing you down. Skate for a while. Then I'll meet you by the refreshment table," she said, pointing.

"Well, okay," he reluctantly agreed. "You still mad at me?"

She shrugged. "Maybe."

She watched him skate away, leaning into the wind. "When I get back, I'll teach you some tricks," he called back.

"Yeah, like how to stay on my skates!" she shouted. She wasn't sure he'd heard her.

A gust of wind ruffled her hair. She pulled her wool ski cap down. She felt sorry she had suspected Luke.

Party pooper, she scolded herself.

"What am I doing way out here?" she asked herself out loud.

The other skaters seemed miles away. She couldn't

even hear the music, only the steady booming of drums, echoing off the trees.

Surrounded by darkness, she felt suddenly afraid.

I've got to get away from here.

I've got to get back to the others.

She started to skate, the ice slushy beneath her skates.

She heard a loud *crack,* spreading across the ice like a soft thunderclap, very nearby.

She tried to skate faster. Lost her balance. Stumbled. Fell onto her stomach.

"Oh, wow. Great party," she muttered sarcastically.

As she pulled herself to her knees, she saw the hooded figure skating toward her.

Who is that? Melissa wondered and climbed all the way to her feet.

The hooded figure was skating fast, bent low, face cloaked in darkness under the hood.

Melissa squinted hard, trying to see who it was.

Closer. Closer. Skating low and fast in a straight line toward Melissa.

And what was that in the skater's hand?

Something that caught the torchlight. Something silvery.

Slender and silvery.

Like a knife blade.

"Ohhh!" Melissa uttered a moan of terror. She tried to scramble away, but her legs wouldn't cooperate.

She slipped, almost fell again.

The ice cracked behind her.

The skater approached, head bent low.

Melissa stared in open-mouthed horror.

The hood flew back. She saw the long red hair fly out from under it.

"Rachel?" she cried.

The skater glided rapidly through the shadows. The arm holding the slender blade rose up.

Melissa struggled to dodge away.

"Rachel!"

Head still lowered, red hair trailing over the fallen hood, she crashed into Melissa without slowing.

"Oh!" Melissa cried out, rocked back by the force of the collision.

And then she gasped as the knife plunged into her side.

Chapter 32

ON THIN ICE

"*S*omebody help me!" Melissa tried to scream. But in her terror, her voice came out a choked murmur.

She waited for the pain to roll up her side.

"Oh!" She realized the knife had plunged into the enormous, bulky overcoat. It had missed her.

Her attacker realized it too, and tugged the knife out of the coat, preparing to thrust it forward again.

"Rachel, *please!*" Melissa shrieked. In her panic, she lost her footing. She started to fall forward.

"Rachel—" As she started to fall, Melissa reached out and clutched at her attacker to hold herself up.

"Oh!" Her hands got tangled in the long red hair— and pulled it off.

A wig.

Stumbling backward, the red wig in both hands, Melissa caught her balance.

"Erica!" she cried. "You!"

Erica glowered angrily at her through the darkness,

the knife raised at her side. "Give the wig back, Melissa," Erica said, breathing hard, reaching for it with her free hand. "We don't want the Drama Club to miss it, do we?"

"Erica, *why?*" Melissa cried. *"Why?"*

With a violent, angry tug, Erica grabbed the wig from Melissa. Her eyes gleamed furiously at Melissa in the flickering shadows.

"Surprised, Melissa?" she asked through clenched teeth.

"Yes," Melissa admitted.

"Of course. You'd never suspect Erica. You'd never even *think* of Erica. No one ever did," Erica said bitterly. "After all, Melissa, who am I? I'm no one!"

"Erica, please—" Melissa pleaded as Erica raised the knife once again.

"Rachel is the beautiful one," Erica continued, ignoring Melissa's cry. "And Josie was the popular one. And me? I was *poor Erica,* so plain, so shy, so *ordinary."*

She lowered the knife and skated closer, her breath steaming up in front of her. Melissa tried to back up, but the ice behind her was starting to crack.

I've got to keep Erica talking, Melissa thought desperately. It's my only chance. "You—you killed Josie?" she asked.

"Of course!" Erica replied in a raspy whisper.

Melissa gasped. "Your own sister? Erica, *why?"*

"Josie had to die," Erica whispered. "She was responsible for Rachel's accident. But did she take any responsibility? No. Josie went on with her life as if nothing had happened. And me—I was stuck with Rachel."

She thrust her face close to Melissa's, her eyes seething with anger. "Do you know how many lives were ruined the day of Rachel's accident, Melissa? Do you know how many? Two! Rachel's and mine. Ruined forever. But you and Josie were just fine, weren't you? You were just fine."

"That's not true, Erica," Melissa told her heatedly. "Josie and I, we were both—"

"Shut up!" Erica screamed. "Do you know how much I looked forward to high school? Do you have any idea? But thanks to you and Josie, I couldn't enjoy it for a minute. I had to give up everything to take care of Rachel. And Josie gave up nothing. I couldn't let her get away with that. I couldn't."

Melissa gazed past Erica to the crowd of skaters so far away across the ice. Where is Luke? she wondered. Where is he?

"But the valentines," she told Erica. "I don't understand. Dave sent Josie those threatening valentines. And you—"

"When Dave started sending those awful valentines, I saw my chance to kill Josie," Erica revealed, her eyes glowing in the darkness, her face close to Melissa's as if challenging Melissa to back away. "Those valentines gave me the idea. I knew when I saw them I could pay Josie back for ruining my life, for ruining Rachel's life. And I could get away with it."

"But you were stabbed too!" Melissa exclaimed.

"I stabbed myself," Erica said in her raspy whisper. "It was easy compared to the pain I already felt."

"I don't believe it," Melissa blurted out, shaking her head.

Where is Luke? Where is anybody? Doesn't anybody see us out here?

"I was home, pretending to be too upset to go to Josie's funeral," Erica recalled. "I was worried about being caught, about people figuring out that I had killed Josie. Then I saw Dave break into our house. Dave to the rescue again. He was giving me the perfect chance to throw all suspicion off me. I called the police. Then I stabbed myself without even thinking about it. I knew Dave would rescue me before I lost too much blood." She snickered. "Good old Dave."

"But you killed Dave too?" Melissa cried, horrified by her own words. "You killed him last week!"

"I had to. He was figuring things out. He realized I still had the valentines he sent to Josie. He realized I was using them to copy his handwriting on the cards I sent to you."

Melissa slid back a few inches. The ice cracked noisily.

Laughter floated across the ice from the skaters near the shore.

I've got to get past her and skate to the others, Melissa thought. *I've got to!*

Erica raised the knife as if reading Melissa's thoughts. "Enough talk," she said quietly.

"But why me?" Melissa cried shrilly, a wave of panic tightening her chest. "I've been your friend, Erica."

Erica uttered a bitter laugh. "You're no friend," she said. "You got everything, Melissa. Poor Rachel lost everything. You even got Luke. You even took Luke away from Rachel. And that made *me* even more of a prisoner—because after you took Luke away, I was all that Rachel had left."

She let the wig drop at her feet and raised the knife. "You have to die, Melissa. It's only fair. You killed Rachel and me. Now you have to die too."

"Why the wig?" Melissa demanded desperately, raising her hands as if to shield herself. "Why did you wear the red wig, Erica?"

Erica glanced down at the ball of hair. "This is Rachel's revenge too," she said quietly. "I wanted Rachel to be here too. In some way, she's here with me, getting her revenge on you."

"You're crazy!" Melissa cried. The words burst out of her mouth. "I'm sorry, Erica, but you're crazy!"

Erica uttered an angry curse. The knife swung wildly, cutting the darkness with a near-silent *whoosh* of air.

Melissa stumbled back and saw Luke. He was leaning low, skating rapidly toward her.

"Luke! Help!" she screamed.

Erica thrust the knife at Melissa's throat.

Melissa heard a booming peal of thunder. It took her a few seconds to realize that the sound wasn't thunder. It was the ice cracking beneath them.

"Help me, Luke!" she managed to scream as the ice gave way and she felt herself begin to drop.

She saw Erica's angry expression turn to fear. Erica raised both arms and cried out in terror.

Both girls were screaming as the ice split apart and they dropped into the freezing water.

Chapter 33

DROWNED

Melissa felt the shock of the cold water as she started to sink.

She reached up with her hands. "Luke!"

Lying on his stomach, Luke grabbed for her, capturing both her hands in his. He pulled.

"Luke, help!"

With a loud groan, he slid her up out of the dark hole. The force of his tug sent her scooting on her stomach across the ice.

As she slid, Melissa looked back and saw Luke grab for Erica.

Too late.

Erica slipped down under the tossing waters as if being sucked under.

"I did it all for you, Rachel!" Melissa heard Erica shriek.

And then she disappeared, down into the icy darkness.

Panting loudly, Melissa pulled herself to her knees.

Her heart thudding in her chest, her entire body trembling from the horror, from the cold, she saw Luke lying down leaning into the hole.

"Erica! Erica!" He called her name again and again.

The ice cracked loudly around them.

Melissa slid over to Luke and lay beside him. "Where is she? Why doesn't she come back up?" she cried in a high-pitched, trembling voice she didn't recognize.

"Erica!" Luke cried. "Erica!"

"Look!" Melissa cried, pointing down.

At first, Melissa thought she saw a fish trapped under the thin sheet of ice.

The mouth appeared first, the lips slightly parted.

But then the nose appeared. A human nose.

And then two wide-open eyes.

And Melissa realized to her horror that she was staring down at Erica's face. Erica's face under the ice, pressed up against it, gazing blankly up at them.

"Why doesn't she move? Why doesn't she swim out from under there?" Melissa cried hysterically, gripping Luke's arm. "Why is she staring up at us like that? She isn't moving at all!"

"I don't think she *wants* to come up," Luke said quietly.

Melissa stared in horror at the unmoving, wide-eyed face staring up at her, pressed up against the ice.

Erica has been in a prison for a year, staring out at the world, Melissa thought grimly.

Now she's staring up at us from another prison.

Raising her eyes from the ghastly floating face,

215

Melissa was shocked to see that a crowd of kids had gathered around them. Hushed voices murmured all around.

"What's happening?"

"Did Melissa fall?"

"Is someone in the water?"

"Did the ice break?"

"Go get help."

"Somebody—get help!"

With a sigh, Luke backed up and climbed to his feet and helped Melissa up. He put his arm firmly around her waist and, holding her tightly, started to lead her away.

Looking down, Melissa suddenly realized she was gripping the red wig in her hand.

"Ohh." With a near-silent cry, she tossed the wig to the ice, as if tossing away all the horror of the night. Then she buried her face in Luke's jacket as they skated away.

Chapter 34

A ROMANTIC IDEA

"*I* made this," Rachel said, smiling.

Melissa and Luke leaned forward on the couch and studied the painting Rachel held up in front of her. "A snowman—right?" Melissa guessed.

"Right!" Rachel said, laughing gleefully. "It's a snowman."

Mrs. McClain watched from near the den doorway, leaning against the wall, a pleased smile on her face.

"Well, that's a good painting," Luke told Rachel.

"I paint a lot at school," Rachel said, lowering the painting to her lap. As she started to roll it up, her smile faded, replaced by a thoughtful expression. "I wish I could show it to Erica," she said wistfully.

"Yes," Melissa said awkwardly, glancing at Luke. Luke was staring at his watch.

"I miss my sister," Rachel said, rolling up the painting. "But I'm going to get better. I'm going to get better and go outside by myself."

"Yes, you are," Mrs. McClain said with forced enthusiasm. She crossed the room and stepped up behind the couch, placing her hands on Rachel's shoulders. "But I think Melissa and Luke want to leave now."

"Yes, we're late," Luke said, jumping to his feet.

Melissa bent over Rachel and hugged her. "I'll come visit you soon."

"I'm going to paint another snowman," Rachel told her.

Melissa and Luke said goodbye to Mrs. McClain and showed themselves out. They stepped into a blustery March day, a thin layer of snow on the ground, high white clouds floating in a blue sky.

"That was a good visit," Melissa said, taking Luke's hand as they made their way down the driveway and headed across the street to her house. "I haven't seen Rachel since—since Valentine's Day, I guess. Three weeks."

"Don't mention Valentines' Day," Luke muttered. "What a horrible holiday."

"Yeah, you're right," Melissa agreed wistfully. A gust of wind ruffled her hair. She leaned against Luke as they walked. "You know what? Next year let's forget about Valentine's Day and send each other Groundhog's Day cards."

Luke stopped at the bottom of the driveway and kissed her. "Groundhog's Day cards," he repeated. "What a romantic idea . . ."

About the Author

R. L. STINE doesn't know *where* he gets the ideas for his scary books! But he wants to assure worried readers that none of the horrors of FEAR STREET ever happened to him in real life.

Bob lives in New York City with his wife, Jane, and twelve-year-old son, Matt. He is the author of more than two dozen bestselling mysteries and thrillers for Young Adult readers.

In addition to his publishing work, he is Head Writer of the children's TV show "Eureeka's Castle," seen on Nickelodeon.

THE NIGHTMARES
NEVER END . . .
WHEN YOU VISIT

FEAR STREET®

Next . . . *THE CHEATER*

Carter Phillips is under a lot of pressure from her father to do well on her math achievement test—so much pressure that she convinces math genius Adam Messner to take the test for her . . . in exchange for one date. But Adam wants more than a date. Much more. Carter knows that if she doesn't give Adam whatever he wants, he'll tell her secret and ruin her life. She's desperate to get rid of him. Is murder the only way out?